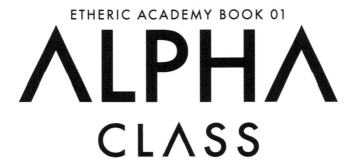

ETHERIC ACADEMY BOOK 01

ALPHA
CLASS

TS PAUL
MICHAEL ANDERLE

COPYRIGHT

DEDICATION

From Michael

To Family, Friends and
Those Who Love
To Read.
May We All Enjoy Grace
To Live The Life We Are
Called.

From Scott Paul

To my wife, Heather Paul

Alpha Class - The Etheric Academy Book 01
Team Includes

Beta Readers

Dorene Johnson (US Navy (Ret) & DD)
Diane Velasquez (Chinchilla Lady & DD)

Editors
Kat Lind
Stephen Russell

JIT Beta Readers - From both of us, our deepest gratitude!
Sherry Foster
Maria Stanley
Keith Kell
Wayne Johnson
David Williamson
Aidan Shanahan
Michael Pendergrass

Mark Katz
Philip R. Slocum
Brent Bakkan
Lori Harris Smith
John Raisor
Scott McDougall
Brent Smith
Brian Douglas Fennell
Lynn F. Ten Eyck
Ebhdoc Ebhdoc
Christine Stewart
Dean Agnew
Robin Stonecipher

*If I missed anyone, **please** let us know!*

CHAPTER ONE

QBBS Meredith Reynolds

Bethany Anne was eating in the common cafeteria. Her area was a little offset from most, allowing a few feet of extra space for her guards to react. Marcus wasn't frisked before he approached her table. "My Queen, I mean Bethany Anne, may I have a moment?" Marcus Cambridge was a bit frantic, which got her attention right away.

She raised an eyebrow and set her tablet aside, "Marcus, what's wrong?" She tried to avoid reading the minds of her oldest friends.

"What is this memo I just received about teaching a class?" He was holding out his tablet, shaking it, "I asked Bobcat but he was laughing too hard to tell me. Since it came from your office, I was hoping that you might be able to provide some answers."

Smiling, she decided to break it to him ever so gently. "That is a reminder about the Etheric Academy. You are slated as one of the primary instructors."

Marcus stood up straighter and looked from her to the tablet and then to her. "Academy? As in students? When did I sign up for that?" He looked back at the document, his eyes searching the words again for another clue.

Bethany Anne put her elbow on the table and laid her chin in her cupped hand, "If you remember, it was actually your idea, to begin with. We were laying out the basic outline for the Meredith Reynolds, and you said it would be great if we had some sort of science academy to train up our people. I took your basic concept and implemented it."

She opened her arms wide, with a smile gracing her face and a gleam in her eye. "Surprise!"

Marcus's face scrunched up. "I don't remember saying anything like that." He stood there a moment, "Damn Bobcat and his drinking parties!" He turned to her, a look of resignation on his face, "So, I have to lecture or something?"

Bethany Anne couldn't hold in her humor any longer. She shook her head and laughed just a little. "Not quite. ADAM pull up the academy layout for Marcus, please."

The wall behind Bethany Anne lit up with a full-color graphic design layout of the academy, built inside the Asteroid base, Meredith Reynolds. "We tested all of the children, both Wechselbalg and human alike. The tests were hard since TOM and ADAM came up with some of the questions. Only the best of the best were good enough for this first trial. They needed to already be excelling in regular school and have a desire to advance themselves for the greater good."

She reached for her fork, "We had thirty students pass the first time."

Marcus's eyes opened wide. "Thirty? I have to teach *thirty*?" Marcus was starting to panic.

She put up a hand, "We have broken them up into groups of five. We mixed personalities and skills to make each group a possible working team. Using a block schedule, they will each spend six weeks on a topic or skill. What you will teach them is ultimately up to you. You will get them all, eventually. But only five at any one time."

"Oh. I guess there was a memo or something that I missed?" Marcus blushed a little bit.

"There was. Do I need to assign assistants down in the lab for you? Do not use the kids for that. I want them to learn stuff, not play 'fetch the left-handed wrench' because it's funny."

He nodded his head, his eyes getting his now infamous thinking look. "I think we can come up with some things to do." He returned his focus to Bethany Anne, "What else are they learning?"

Bethany Anne shrugged and started counting on a hand, "Orbital mechanics, navigation, engineering, weapons and tactics, flight controls," she closed the hand and started counting off again. "Logistics, space walking, computers and programming to begin with. We plan to add a few other skill sets as we go, including genetics, negotiation, and survival." She looked at him, "These children are our future. Remember, we will be leaving Earth behind. They need to learn these skills."

He put up a hand, "Oh, I agree!" He looked to be concentrating on something. "This was really my idea?"

"It was. You wanted Tina to have a place to learn that didn't involve Earth and NASA."

Marcus started backing up, "Good ... I think ... OK, then. Thank you, my Queen, I can make this work." He turned around and bumped into a chair, never seeming to notice.

Bethany Anne waited until the scientist was out the door before breaking out in laughter. She turned to her guard, "Did he really not know?"

John Grimes had a look of disbelief on his face. "I think Bobcat may have neglected to tell him due to some sort of bet."

Bethany Anne cocked her head to one side, then slowly nodded. "Yes, that is what ADAM says as well."

"That I can believe." John turned around to stare at the academy layout. "Is everything ready to go, down there, for this?"

"They keep saying it is. Your niece was accepted, you know." She stabbed at some green beans with her fork, "I have an obligation to make sure she gets whatever she needs to succeed."

The large man nodded his head. "I remember. Too bad Todd didn't qualify. He hasn't completely come around to our way of thinking, yet."

"He'll get there. Tweedle Dee and Tweedle Dum tell me he is obsessed with aircraft and spaceships right now. Maybe you can give him a nudge in the right direction." She put a forkful of food in her mouth as ADAM and TOM bitched in her mind about her using Tabitha's nicknames for Hirotoshi and Ryu.

"Maybe I can." The big man stared off into space for a moment.

Carefully checking the list, Tina placed each item in the bag.

She really didn't need to check. When her mom told her about her acceptance into the Etheric Academy, she studied the information completely. The Etheric Academy was the brainchild of Queen Bethany Anne, Marcus, and two sisters that were rescued by the Guard several years ago.

Her mom had introduced her to them at one of the casual dinners those inside the inner circle occasionally had. They had worked to overcome Michael's mental suggestions to forget the battle they had been a part of, which was pretty miraculous for regular non-upgraded humans.

"Tina, I don't want you to go," her brother admitted, playing with a pencil she had on her desk.

"You'll get an invite too, Todd. We took the same tests together." Tina's brother was only now starting to come around to the fact that this was it.

Their future was in space.

He looked up to her, "I'll miss you."

Smiling at her brother, Tina gave him a gentle shove. "I'm just going to the other side of the Meredith Reynolds, you know. It's not like I'm going back to Earth or something!"

"I know that! It's just…" He sat on her bed and hung his head.

Tina gave her brother another shove. "Cheer up, you get the whole room to yourself now." The two of them shared a small room about half the size of a shipping container. Cheryl Lynn actually got one of the first apartments on the Meredith Reynolds to be built. She helped set the standard size limits.

Todd looked around the small room, seeing the possibilities. He might be able to fit one of the new pod simulators in here. He would have to ask Mom first, though.

He spoke as his mind reviewed the possibilities in the new space, "Be careful over there. Some of those Russian kids are big."

She shook her head, "I'll be fine. They are trying really

hard to fit in. You just have to give them a chance. I know you like Yurgi. I've seen you two discussing aircraft profiles and flight navigation mathematics."

Todd turned his focus back to Tina, "That is different. Yurgi is just a little guy. He's not like some of those really big guys!"

Tina shook her head at her brother. She wondered if his attitude might be what was holding him back. "Those big guys are Wechselbalg kids, so they are supposed to be a bit larger. You need to figure out what you really want, Todd. Do you want to work for a living or lead? When you figure it out, that will be when the Academy admits you. Wait and see."

She put the last item in the carryall bag and slung it over her shoulder. "Come on. Mom said something about a special dinner."

The two siblings opened the connecting hatch door and resealed it behind them. The asteroid base was reasonably secure, but safety procedures needed to be learned. Better to learn them now, rather than when lives were on the line.

Sniffing the air Tina smiled. "Pizza!"

Coming into the kitchen area, Cheryl Lynn smiled at her two teenage children, "There you two are! Tina, I have your favorite for you." Two steaming pizzas sat in the center of the small table in the dining area.

Cheese pizza done right was an exquisite experience. It was the purest form of pizza or at least that is what Tina believed. The two pizzas had a familiar odor, and she looked at her mom in shock then back to the Giuseppe's boxes. Where the smell had come from … too many miles away to figure out now. "How?"

Cheryl Lynn smiled. "Earth isn't all that far away, you know. I got Giuseppe's special just for you."

Practically diving into the pizza, the kids each grabbed one of the massive slices.

Giuseppe's was a family favorite back in Dallas before their father left them. They could never afford to go there after that. This made the day all that much more special. Tina got up and walked over to her mother, enveloping her parent in her arms, a tiny tear just at the edge of her eye.

In another part of the huge station, several other students were getting ready. Maxim and Nestor were cousins. They had been a part of the evacuation of the town of Romon-avka. They were Wechselbalg, as were most of their immediate family. Nestor's father Leonid was training to become a Guardian.

He wanted more for both his son and nephew.

Leonid was pointing to both boys, his Russian accent full of pride, "You need to go to the school. We swore to follow the Queen in all things. You both took the tests and passed them. Maxim, your father, would want this for you. You know it. He wanted a better life for you. It's why he stayed to fight."

The big man looked at his own son. "You too Nestor. We talked of this. Your wolf is not the strongest, yet. These people can teach you things and let you do things that will make you the best of us. Trust them. Now go pack the both of you." He pointed at the door to their room.

The two started towards the room.

"He has a point, Nestor." Maxim was older and wiser. Or at least he thought so.

"Did I ask you for your opinion?" The smaller Wechsel-balg growled at his cousin.

"Fine, whatever. We need to pack." Maxim pulled out a couple of small bags and began throwing clothes into them.

Nestor stared at his cousin and sighed. "Give me one of those." He grabbed a bag and started to pack.

Today was the first day of the rest of his life.

The young woman stood there, her hand on her cocked hip, "Papa, I don't wish to go to this Academy. I should stay here and help you."

Her father looked down at his headstrong daughter, "We have discussed this, Yana. We are no longer in the Motherland, and our family may never return. I know we raised you to be proud of your heritage by telling you stories of a time lost in the past. That is my fault. The Konstantinovich family will no longer hide in the shadows dreaming empire dreams. We lost our chance at the throne of Russia during the revolution." Nicholas waved his arms around him. "Our future and that of our family lie out there. To get there, you need to do this."

"But Papa…" she started again.

His eyes flashed just a little more firmly, "Nyet! No. It is done. The servants of Queen Bethany Anne have told us you passed the test with one of the highest percentile scores. You will go, and you will learn what you have to know. Forge your own path, daughter." He smiled and walked towards the kitchen. Yana stood staring at her father, ground her teeth together, then walked to the front door, trying to slam it on her way out of the house.

House! The apartment wasn't what she wished in her life. She had dreamed of palaces her entire life as her family shuttled her around to hide her from first Soviet and then Russian assassins and the Cheka.

Her family was everything to her. She walked the hallways of the Meredith Reynolds and stared out some of the armored windows at the emptiness of space. It wasn't fair sometimes. She could remember her father coming and telling her that he had sworn to another.

That wasn't the worst! The Cheka was coming, and the entire town would have to evacuate on foot if need be. They had to leave everything that their family had toiled for almost a century to build.

She watched as several construction drones and maintenance crews worked outside, in space. She bet they didn't have to burn down their entire lives just to escape those that wanted to kill them. Everything was too easy up here.

Shaking her head, she walked back towards her family's home.

The door made a whooshing noise as it opened, she called out. "Father, are you still here?" She closed the hatch behind her and locked it.

"Did you have a good walk?" Nicholas smiled at her expression. "Better shut your mouth or flies might land there." He was sitting at the table studying a tablet.

Her mouth snapped shut as he continued. "It's what you do every time you need to work out a problem. Your mother was the same way." Her father had a sad, misty expression on his face.

"You rarely speak of her."

"She was a beautiful woman, your mother. You favor her." He reached out and stroked Yana's hair. "If she were still alive, she would want you to better yourself. Trust your instincts. Embrace the future, Yana."

He sat back down and picked up his tablet again.

Yana's lips pressed together, "Do you still have the list of requirements?"

"It's in your room. You are making the correct decision. I'm proud of you."

The list was where he said it would be. Yana packed swiftly, the instructions gave a time for the shuttle to pick up the students and she had less than an hour.

Ronnie Diamantz was enjoying the ride so far. It still amazed him that werewolves and vampires were actually real.

His father didn't keep him sheltered, but he hadn't explained much to Ronnie. However, the other kids did talk.

His parents were into computers like he was into science. They were so easily distracted by bits and bytes. Not him, give him chemical reactions anytime.

The Meredith Reynolds was huge! He had never been in this residential section before and was enjoying the tram ride. If he were more mechanically inclined, he would be interested in the electromagnetic propulsion system that the tiny train employed to shuttle groups around the asteroid.

To him, it was just a cool looking car. Every seat was filled by kids like him. He had already spotted several Wechselbalg and some of the Russian kids. Maybe they would be in his class.

Ronnie looked forward to this school, this was going to be a freaking blast!

CHAPTER TWO

QBBS Meredith Reynolds, Academy Area

A re you ready for this?"

Diane looked at her twin sister and smiled. "Why would I not be? It's not like fighting off Forsaken in the wilds of Turkey. These are just children. Besides," she looked around at the stone walls, running a hand across the smooth surface as they walked along. "We helped build this place."

Dorene agreed. "That's true. I'm still getting used to having the energy to even think of tackling something like this."

The hall the two ladies were walking through led from the administrative offices to the entrance of the school. The Meredith Reynolds was a massive asteroid that TQB had turned into a base, well a base station, actually.

When Bethany Anne had found the two sisters, they were on the run from more than one Government. Many years ago they took a sponsored trip to Turkey. They helped children enjoy a foreign country and saw the sights themselves, and in return, they had been able to save a few dollars.

What actually happened, was they ended up trapped in a cave with a bunch of kids. Everyone hiding from ravenous Nosferatu that were trying to kill them.

TQB intervened, led by the Queen herself. The two sisters' memories were altered so they would forget the entire incident. However, something unexpected happened, and they both woke up one morning with the memories returned to them.

Dorene tried to discreetly find out more information about the event, not realizing who was involved at the time, or how badly information about Bethany Anne was wanted. Computer records were useless. They only glossed over the event, calling it a meteor strike. Digging deeper into public records and contacting a few friends from her time in the service punched in names she remembered. Names like Ecaterina, Gabrielle, and Bethany Anne.

Her search touched off a twin hunt of sorts, which led the two to need to choose between joining TQB in space, or ending up lost down a hole with a government on Earth. ADAM found them before anyone else and sent the Queen's Marines to save them.

Anyone that had any sort of connection to Queen Bethany Anne and to TQB was wanted by many governments of the world for interrogation. Information of any kind was very valuable.

Their information, since it was so far back, was unique.

"Why do you say that? Some of this was your idea. Well, yours and that cutie, Marcus." Diane was enjoying the revitalization that came with the job. The two elderly ladies no longer looked their age.

PAUL AND ANDERLE

They, like many here on the station, had been put through a medical pod which modified their bodies with nanocytes, providing them not only a more youthful body, but also enhanced energy.

"Some of it was my idea. The Queen had her say as well. Especially when it came to that." She pointed upwards to the wall. In large, foot-high letters was a quote from the Queen herself. Bethany Anne hadn't remembered saying it, but it was verified by TOM, the Kurtherian alien.

"As long as a student pushes themselves, I'll turn over the heavens to help them. - Bethany Anne"

"I like that one the most." The two women agreed. There were others scattered around the school.

Diane looked over to Dorene, "Did the dorms get set up OK?"

She answered, "They did. The engineering crew said the rooms are all the width of two cargo containers. I have the sexes divided for now. Later we can discuss mixing them if there aren't any issues. At least most of the Russian kids are used to doubling up. Personal modesty sort of goes out the window when dealing with Wechselbalg. If the kids can handle it, we may let the groups team up that way."

"How many girls did we get?"

"Not as many as we hoped for. Too much coddling is what I think. The Queen and Gabrielle make excellent role models, but the hard sciences weren't stressed in school for these kids. Tina was the exception to the rule. There are a few others as well."

Diane glared at her sister, "So, again, how many are girls?"

Dorene smiled, "Oops, sorry. We have ten girls and twenty boys. Twelve are Wechselbalg of various ages and pack status. About half come to us as refugees from Romonavka along with ten Russian human children. The rest are from the Colorado base. It's too bad we didn't remember meeting the Queen and her troops until recently. The base there sounds like it's pretty cool."

Diane shook her head, "Let's worry about the school first; you can chase pod pilots later." Dorene had a big smile on her face. Another good thing about having the years wiped from your body was the ability to chase sexy men.

Sexy men that were pilots.

Dorene looked around, "Right. So, the dorms are set and have been furnished. Technical Engineering supplied tablets for all the students along with locator beacons. At the moment, they will wear them. Once they finish school, they will be able to have them implanted like many of the regular crew."

"Good. That sounds good. Bethany Anne wants you to take care of student welfare." Diane held up her hands in a stopping motion. "Before you start, this comes from the Queen herself. I have to take student administration. Maybe we can switch later. Many of these kids have never been away from home for extended periods. We need to be there for them to lean on."

"If I have to. You know their parents are only a few miles away on the other side of the asteroid." Dorene pointed upward.

Diane shrugged, "I know that, and you know that, but most of them don't know it, or if they do, they don't know it emotionally yet. Besides, we are supposed to teach them to be independent. No running home to mom. If that happens, we need to track it carefully. They might not be up to the task for the crew we want anyway. Try to get them to listen to you. These kids are the future of the realm."

PAUL AND ANDERLE

Diane smiled at her sister. "Come on, the train should be arriving soon. Have any of the trainers arrived in the great hall?"

"I have no idea. I can check, though." Dorene looked up and called out to the operations E.I. (Entity Intelligence) for the Meredith Reynolds herself. "Meredith? Have the instructors arrived for introductions and sorting?"

The E.I.'s voice resonated around them, coming from discreet speakers, "Hello, Dorene. The representatives from most of the departments are waiting for you and your sister in the main hall. The Queen along with her bodyguard will arrive in your office moments before commencement. Please be sure the room is empty."

"It is. I activated the special lock and everything." Dorene said, then paled for a moment.

Diane looked concerned as she noticed her sister's face, "DJ, are you alright?"

Dorene looked around, a little frantic, "I just remembered that I left out a few items on the desk." She turned to her sister, "Maybe the Queen's guards won't notice?"

"What did you leave out?" Diane relaxed, she had an idea where this was heading.

"Remember those calendars we found on the Internet?" Dorene blushed.

Diane just shook her head. "Only you. Maybe they won't notice. But, leave John alone. Remember what happened last time? We need both you and Jean. She almost ejected you out of that port last time you got frisky."

"That woman scares the crap out of me! It was just a little pinch. Who knew she was tapped into the security system?"

"If anyone could be, it would be her. No touchy-touchy

the big guard man this time, OK?" Dorene nodded her head in agreement. Jean had her pressed up against the supposed waste ejection port last time with her hand on the release button.

It had taken some serious fast talking to get Dorene out of that one. Gabrielle had asked the sisters if they needed to join a twelve-step program for women who pinched men's butts.

The sisters continued to bicker at each other until they reached the double doors at the end of the hall. Above the door was another quote. This one was from Albert Einstein. "The true sign of intelligence is not knowledge, but *imagination*."

Inside the auditorium, a man – a scientist, one would guess based on his clothes– was speaking to two others. One woman was considerably shorter than he, the other a man in a suit. The scientist had one arm gesticulating wildly, "… and I'm telling you, it was a brilliant idea. We need this sort of thing for when we go through the gate into the next universe. Who knows what we will find there? And, it's a one-way trip! If we don't educate the kids now using the resources we have available here in this system, we will be harming them, not helping them. Earth still has much we can teach them. But it must be us, not those idiots back there. Especially not those guys at NASA."

While he practically towered over her, the lady didn't give up one inch in the discussion, "Marcus, NASA aside, do you really think that we should take time out of our busy schedules to teach? I have a ton of work to do. We have weapons to build and systems that don't even exist, yet we need to create. My area is way behind, according to my schedule. All of this is going to screw up my system so much." This time, it was the Primary of the Research and Development group waving her hands all about.

"Not just your system, Jean. My boys are working full out on ship design and finishing this." Jeo waved his arm for emphasis, like a conductor for a band. "We have a ton of work to do and not much time." He looked around in frustration, "Hell, I'm losing productivity just standing here."

"Why don't you folks just take a chill pill?" Everyone turned to see Captain Thomas standing at the edge of the stage. "What? You don't think I'm hip to new phrases? Some of my new crew told me to say that." He looked around the auditorium, "This Academy is a good thing."

He pointed to the scientist, "None of you, except Marcus, are thinking of the big picture. We gave intelligence and mechanical tests to young people. Our young people. They are our future crew members, workers, and maybe leaders. We need them, and they need us to teach them what we know. Think of them as interns. Each selected department will get five new interns every six weeks. I will tell you now, I can think of lots of scut work and some real projects that an extra five sets of hands would be really helpful. These young adults are the cream of the crop. Some of them might be able to help on levels that we can't even imagine yet."

The man paused a moment before adding, "Besides, this is what Bethany Anne wants. So grow a pair and straighten up."

The arguing department heads frowned almost in unison and nodded their heads. He had a point. They all heard clapping and turned to look at the back of the auditorium.

"Thank you, Captain. That was well done. Is everyone ready? The students will be here soon." Diane and her sister walked down the aisle toward the stage.

"You ladies are as fetching as ever." The Captain had a big smile on his face as he helped the two new school administrators up to the stage.

"Thank you," Diane shook his hand and turned toward the others. "And once again, to everyone here, thank you all for coming."

The others greeted her with nods and other acknowledgments. Jean gave Dorene the evil eye, but smiled at the same time.

She pointed to the doors in the back of the auditorium. "Thirty children will be arriving through those doors in a few minutes. Our goal here is to train for the future, or all the work we have done is worthless. Once we go through the gate, the kids become our resource pool. My sister and I understand that, and so does the Queen. Arguments aside, we need all of you to be on board with us, too." The two twins looked around the stage at the department heads. Several monitors showed the faces or offices of those that couldn't be present physically. "Are you?"

There was a pause before a new voice entered the conversation.

"That is a question I would like the answer to as well." Everyone on stage turned toward Bethany Anne's voice.

The Queen strode onto the stage from the direction of the admin offices. Her ever-present white German Shepherd, Ashur, and John Grimes, her bodyguard, followed in her wake. She was dressed as if she was either returning from or going into an operation. She had on black leather with pistols and two swords.

PAUL AND ANDERLE

John Grimes looked in all directions without turning his head more than ten degrees. He knew everyone on stage, but it didn't hurt to be cautious.

He tried not to smile at the twin sisters because Jean wouldn't like it. Inside he was laughing his ass off. It had been a few years, and he had forgotten about the calendars the women had put together of him and the rest of the Queen's Bitches. All of the guys had joined in, to make the beefcake calendar.

He wondered where and how they found them. Bethany Anne had poked him in the arm and pointed when she first saw them, smirking.

Everyone on stage nodded and voiced agreement with the woman who started this grand adventure they were on. She was the reason for everything, and they owed her the world.

"Good. We need this to work. Ladies?" Bethany Anne looked at the newest additions to her group.

Diane stepped past her sister, who was trying pitifully to hide from both John and Jean, to answer Bethany Anne, "The children should be coming through the doors in just a moment. Max, the shuttle driver, just dropped them off."

CHAPTER THREE

This is it! The Etheric Academy. Be sure you gather up your belongings, my next stop is waste management, and trust me, you don't want to go there looking for stuff." Max was the tram driver. The internal trains were mostly automatic, except when it came to those for the Academy. Both the Queen and the school administrators felt a human presence would be best.

Max peered at his monitors and readouts. "Hey, you in the back? Are you awake? This is your stop." Pressing a few buttons, the lights in the last car began to strobe and flash. Anyone still in there was awake now. He watched carefully and shook his head as a slightly-built young man stepped off the car tentatively. "Kids."

He double checked to make sure the cars were all clear and exited the cockpit himself. The tram would return to regular service unless needed for students. Here at the Academy, Max was the all-around Mr-Fixit. His job was to keep the place running and do any heavy lifting the Administrators needed.

WEEEET. Max pulled his fingers out of his mouth. Not many people remembered how to whistle like that anymore. The new students all stopped and turned to look at him, their eyes wide.

"Gather round," he waited for the kids to get closer. A couple stepped back to make room for their shorter classmates. Max pointed to the main doors, "Now, those are the doors to your new life. If anyone wishes to return to your family, now is the time to speak up. There is no shame in wanting to wait." None of the kids spoke, but many looked around like prairie dogs searching for predators.

"Great. This is your new beginning. Go through the doors and hang a left into the auditorium. We have a small presentation set up for you." Smiling, he stepped ahead of the kids and opened the door on the left.

All thirty kids tried to fit through the doors at the same time. There was very little pushing or shoving, just everyone trying to squeeze in at once.

"Take your time. The school isn't going anywhere." *Kids were the same everywhere*, Max thought to himself. He had been a building maintenance supervisor for some of the biggest colleges in the country before answering an email that appeared on his phone at home one night. That had been the best decision of his life.

Who wouldn't want to work in space?

The main lobby of the Etheric Academy was a work of art. A swirling three-dimensional representation of the galaxy floated across the ceiling. It was continually being updated by the command center. Unknown to any of the staff, it was one of the backup navigational displays for the crew of the

ALPHA CLASS

Meredith Reynolds. The asteroid's designers didn't believe in keeping all their eggs in one basket.

Redundancy and resiliency were the mantras, safety the results.

Carved staircases rose from the floor and arched in two directions. Each leading to a different part of the school. A hallway extended out between the staircases. It led to the admin offices as well as the small clinic.

Max squeezed past the large group of Wechselbalg and Russians lingering at the doors. "This is the main hall. Up those stairs to the right are the dorms. The left is classrooms and a few other specialty rooms. Down there is the Administrative offices, my office, and our small clinic. A word to the wise."

He waved his hands and held up a single finger. "Do not, under any circumstances, irritate or disrespect Dr. Running Wolf. She has volunteered to assist us here. Anyone who causes trouble will answer to me. Now, go through those doors over there." Max had to jump out of the way as he was almost trampled by the enthusiastic kids.

Upon entering, the first thing the new students saw was the Queen! She stood in the middle of the podium in a restful pose. At her side was Ashur, the enormous German Shepherd along with the ever-present John Grimes. Behind her stood an array of other well-known faces. A who's who of the command staff.

"He's huge!"

"OMG! It's the Queen herself!"

"Dude, check out the size of that dog."

"How does someone that size even find clothes?"

The new students filed in and took seats in front of the stage. Bethany Anne heard their comments, and in a few cases, the comments running through their minds and smiled.

John, where do you buy your clothes from?

I have them specially made just for me by a trio of honest-to-God tailors who asked to join us. They have quarters down on level five. John sent his mental-only answer back to his Queen.

Why would tailors choose to go into space? Bethany Anne scrutinized her most loyal bodyguard.

John blushed and answered his Queen and friend. *I may have mentioned to them that the boys and I were leaving Earth and not coming back. Our suits alone put their kids through college.*

Bethany Anne shook her head at him. I should have expected that.

The last of the new students were seated as Bethany Anne walked to the front of the podium. "Welcome to the new Etheric Academy. I'll make this brief, so listen carefully this first time."

She started walking about the stage, moving back and forth. "You have been selected from thousands of applicants to be the first students here. This Academy is something of an experiment. We need special people to help us in our shared goals. We fight to give Earth a choice in its path and to protect it while it chooses. We fight to maintain our existence and our place in the Universe. The graduates of this academy will be special in many ways. You will have the skills that are needed to join with my crew and many of your parents in the fight to save Earth, our way of life, and in many ways, the Universe. You will also be special in that you will understand how to work together to achieve those goals without regard to race, type of modified human you are, or origin."

Bethany Anne stopped and made a gesture towards those

listening attentively in the seats, "There are thirty of you to start this journey, with hundreds more ready in the near future. You are our future, our wealth. We are proud of you and know that you can make a difference."

She continued, "Your classes are designed to quickly get you prepared to be department interns... with a paycheck. The group of you will be broken up into mixed teams of five individuals. Using a rotating block schedule of six weeks, we will teach you what we do to achieve the goals the Empire needs. Work hard and learn quickly!"

Glancing at the people behind her, Bethany Anne made a small hand motion. The twins stepped forward. "These two ladies are the backbone of this school. They will become your mothers and your fathers for the length of your stay here. Trust them with anything that concerns you. You can trust them because I trust them."

Bethany Anne's face grew grim. "The people behind me are to be trusted, too. They are the people who designed and built the pods, shoot the weapons, and fly the ships of our Empire. Each of you will be joining their crews or teams shortly. Learn from them as they will learn from you. You are our hope. We need each other to survive what the future will bring."

Bethany Anne stepped away from the podium and gave a little wave. Ashur and John stepped closer to her, and they all vanished suddenly. The kids in the crowd gave a sudden cry of surprise.

Diane stepped up to the microphone, looking at where Bethany Anne had been just a second ago, before turning back to the kids. "Now that the Queen has gotten your attention, let me introduce a few people here. My name is Diane, and my twin sister, Dorene, is over there. Together with Max, the driver of the tram you came in on, we collectively run this school. We are the ones you come to if you have any sort of problem. If we can't fix it, I'm sure Dr. Running Wolf can." She gestured to a strikingly beautiful woman in a lab coat standing near the stairs.

"Behind me are the heroes of our Empire. Jean Dukes, the master of weapons and destruction. Marcus, the *M* in team BMW. He and the rest of his team have been behind all of the cutting-edge tech advances you see around you. Jeo over there commands the mining and shipbuilding efforts of the Empire."

Diane pointed at the monitors. "ADAM and his computer whiz kids are standing by over there. You will spend six weeks working for, and with, all of these people and more. We have a very full schedule planned for you all. Shortly we will break you up into your teams. These will be your brothers and your sisters for the near future. Teams will do everything but sleep together, for now. When I call your name, you will step forward to receive three things: a school tablet, a locator beacon, and your new assignment."

Diane looked out into the audience and smiled. All she needed now was a floppy old talking hat, and everything would be right with the world.

"Charles Adams." A large boy stood up in the middle of the second row and made his way forward. Diane spoke a few words to him and handed him a tablet. She slipped a wristband over his left hand and pointed toward stage left. Six flags stood there, each bearing a Military designation.

Tina barely noticed when her name was called. She had been studying the words written above the stage. There were quotes and sayings on almost every wall, or at least those she had seen. Many made a lot of sense. The one above her struck home the most for her. "Don't give up, Don't accept mediocrity, Don't accept the status quo." Don't accept the status quo meant the most to her. It reminded her of something John had said around her once or twice. "Don't let the bastards grind you down." She jumped when someone touched her.

"She's calling for you." Tina stared in shock at a tall blond girl with striking blue eyes.

"I'm sorry, what did you say?"

The girl pointed at the stage. "Isn't your name Tina?"

Tina blushed and made her way up to the stage. One of the twins, Diane, handed her a tablet and a bracelet.

"Daydreaming a bit there, kid?"

"I'm sorry."

"It's all good. This tablet is yours. It contains class schedules and other information. The beacon must be worn. Later you can choose to have one implanted, but that is up to you. You have been selected for team Alpha. Please find your flag and stand next to it."

Tina hopped off the stage and ran to her flag as another name was called. With only thirty students, the names were called pretty quickly. Her group grew as two massive Wechselbalg boys were called.

"Hi there, I'm Tina." She held out her hand. Growing up on the base in Colorado she knew lots of Wechselbalg and wasn't afraid of them.

The larger of the two grunted and took her hand. "Nestor." He thumped his chest. Nestor gave the other boy a big shove and called him "Maxim."

More names were called, and Tina recognized a few kids in the other groups. A close few of the students she recognized had been on the scary field trip with her and her brother. The bus had been captured by terrorists in an effort to change the focus from protecting their base, to protecting the kids.

She found herself cheering them on as names were called.

Yana took her tablet and glanced at it as she put it away. The bracelet both confused her and scared her half to death. If the Cheka had something such as this, she might have been killed years ago.

Dorene saw the look of fright on the tall Russian girl's face and instantly knew who she must be. She hurried over to reassure her.

"You're safe here. We promise, Yana. There is no one here that represents what you left, including those who were chasing you."

Yana looked sharply at the young-looking elder. "You know my name?"

"We are aware of everyone's name. You are special. Even the Queen thinks so. We want you to succeed in this."

Fingering the bracelet, Yana nodded. "It's frightening. This could doom my family."

Dorene embraced her and whispered in her ear. "We are your family now dear. To get to you, they would have to go through my sister and me first."

Yana slid the bracelet on and smiled. "Thank you."

"You're welcome. Alpha group is your new class. Go say 'hi' to your new family."

The group looked almost full as she approached them. Tina, the girl she had to wake up, was talking to two Wechselbalg she remembered from the evacuation and long march. A slim waif of a boy stood beside one of the wolves almost hidden by his shadow. The girl named Tina was smiling at her.

"You joining us here in Alpha group?" Yana nodded at her. "Great! Welcome to the family!"

CHAPTER FOUR

Welcome to the family. Such a prophetic thing to hear. Yana took the offered hand and looked at Tina. "Thank you. I'm Yana."

"Nice to meet you, Yana. These two behind me are Maxim and Nestor." Both Wechselbalg boys inclined their heads to her. They knew who she was.

"Who are you?" Yana tapped the smaller boy hiding behind the Weres.

"Sorry, I was watching the other groups. I'm Ronnie or Ron." He held out his pale hand.

Yana took it and looked at the others. "What do all of you do? What I mean to say is, what is your favorite specialty?"

"Science." Tina blurted out then blushed a little. "I love all things having to do with science."

"I like science, but chemistry is my favorite," Ronnie spoke up from behind the group.

PAUL and ANDERLE

"Does that mean you make explosives?" Nestor stared down at the small boy with a strange look on his face. "You blow things up?"

"Not always. Chemistry is just ways of changing matter. It was a materials chemist that helped create this." Ronnie knocked on the wall next to him. "Someone had to figure out how to change natural stone into what looks to be a form of slate. Not something found in space."

"Oh. So, you make bombs." The other Wechselbalg joined in.

"Not really. That would be more Physical chemistry. A general take on chemistry as a whole. My specialty is more Bio and Neurochemistry. I like how chemicals and different reactions affect the body."

"Oooo. Do you get into genetics? Have you read the new book by Cove Bond on the genetics of twins and how they are really one person?" Tina stepped closer.

"I haven't. Is that one new?" Ronnie answered, "The last book I read was about dihydrogen oxide. Did you know it has killed over a hundred thousand people and there is nothing anyone can do about it?"

"Dihydrogen Oxide?" Tina thought for a moment. "Isn't that water?"

"It is! People drown all the time. What genetics books do you have?" Ronnie and Tina moved over closer to the wall and began to speak in a strange scientific language shared only by others in the field and geeks.

Yana watched the two for a while and sighed. "Geeks." She looked over at the two Wechselbalg boys. "What do you two do?"

"Oruzhiye, Batya…"

Yana raised an eyebrow, "English. We are among new

people, and English is what they speak here. We must adapt to the new situation. Now, what were you saying?" Yana looked at the taller of the two Weres.

"Weapons is what I study. My father, Nikolay, stayed behind with Boris to fight those that would kill us. Uncle Leonid has received no word as to what happened to him."

"It is a fine thing, Maxim Nikolayevich, that you have joined the Academy. Much to learn here, I think. Your father would be proud." She turned toward Nestor.

"And you, Nestor Leonidovich, what is it you prefer?"

"I like to drive and fix things. Back home, I repaired cars, trucks, snow machines, and whatever the town needed. Here? I just want to learn more. The past is gone, along with the town." The shorter Were scratched his head.

"That it is, my friends. I have seen the pictures of what is left. What we didn't destroy, the Cheka did for us. Better to stay here in space and start over." Yana looked, and the two science geeks were still at it.

"Hey, the sorting is almost finished." Yana had to wave her hand in front of Ronnie and Tina to get their attention.

Up on stage, Diane finished reading the last name. "Everyone has a new group now. These will be your brothers and sisters for the duration of your time here. Learn from each other and grow stronger because of it. Your tablets contain class schedules, school rules, maps, books, and other learning materials. I encourage all of you to study and interact with your fellow students. The locator beacon is a necessary function here and is non-negotiable. We understand that, for a few of you, having outside forces locate you is a major issue. You don't need to worry about that anymore. The Etheric Realm protects its citizens. I will protect you."

"As will I." Captain Thomas stepped forward.

"And I." All of the others on stage followed him.

"This is what your goal is," she paused, "*learn* all you can."

With a tear in her eye, Diane turned toward the others on stage. "Thank you for your service and support."

Turning back to the six groups, Diane replied. "Now, no more lamentations. Go check out the dorms and the rest of the school if you like. Take the right-hand stairs for the dorms and the left for everything else. Maps in your tablets will get you home." She waved them off.

Five groups ran past the Alpha group at full gallop. Many wished to get the best bunk or check out the flight simulator marked on the map.

Yana stood, hands on her hips watching the two younger group members talk genetics and chemical reactions along with spatial geometry and orbital mechanics. Maxim and Nestor were staring at them, too, but only to decipher what in the hell they were talking about.

"Hey!" The Wechselbalg students looked at her, but not the other two. She motioned at them and glared at Maxim. Sighing loudly, Maxim nudged his cousin, and they each grabbed one of the smaller students and lifted them away from each other.

"What's the big idea?" Tina yelled, twisting in Maxim's arms.

"No fair!" Ronnie added as he glared at Nestor.

Yana shrugged her shoulders, "I thought you wanted to check out the school? My mistake. Put them back, and we will go see if they have any snacks around here, Maxim." The two Wolves started to set Tina and Ronnie back down.

"Wait! What did you say?" Ronnie looked puzzled.

Yana answered, "Didn't you hear? They turned us loose to explore the school. We can follow the map and see some of what they have to offer or go find a good bunk."

Ronnie whipped out his tablet and started searching for information. Yana sighed again.

Geeks.

Tina moved a stray hair out of her eyes, "My mom brought me here when they were building the place. It's pretty cool. They have flight simulators as well as a nice audio-visual library. Mom said they went all out to make it special for us."

Yana looked closer at Tina. "Who is your mother to gain you such access?"

Tina looked around at the mostly empty auditorium, "Cheryl Lynn Grimes. She's the Queen's assistant and acts as her press secretary sometimes. My uncle is John Grimes, one of the Queen's bodyguards. He was the one up there with her on the stage."

Ronnie's mouth dropped open, and the two Wechselbalg perked up. Yana only nodded. "Good. Connections will take you far in any situation. Don't be afraid to use them if needed."

Ronnie asked, "Tina, can you get me John's autograph?"

Tina looked at Ronnie like he was crazy, "His signature? What for?"

Ronnie mumbled, "I collect stuff, that's all."

Tina scrunched up her face a moment, "Ronnie, that doesn't make sense to me. He's here on the base with us all the time. I'll introduce you to him. OK?"

The younger boy nodded his head, but now gazed at Tina with a look of awe.

Yana looked towards the exits, "Let's all go check out the library and the simulators. Then we should try and find good bunks."

Tina held up a small electronic device, "That sounds

great. The library is supposed to have copies of every movie and music track in existence. I want to get some new songs to study by."

"Uh, does that mean we aren't going to the kitchen?" Maxim along with Nestor towered over the two younger students.

Yana's eyebrows came together, "Hungry?"

"We are. Last meal was early morning. Uncle Leonid had Guardian duty." Yana nodded. From what her father had told her, Wechselbalg needed to eat rather frequently.

"Then we check out the cafeteria first. Come along." Taking charge, Yana grabbed the other two humans and nudged the Weres in the proper direction. They went up the ramp and through the doors leading back out to the entrance hall. According to Yana's tablet, the cafeteria should be directly across from the auditorium.

Above the new doors was another quote. "Starve the Ego and Feed the Soul."

Tina stared up at the quote as she passed through the doors. None of this had been in place when she was here during construction. "I'm starting to like this place."

Yana also read the quote and agreed with Tina. She nodded her head as she took in the cafeteria. It was big, bigger than what would be needed for thirty students. This fact told her one thing: these people planned big and intended for the school to grow.

The heaviest looking man she had seen yet on this asteroid peeked around the corner as the doors opened. "Hello, welcome to The End of the Line."

Line? What line? Yana looked around the nearly empty room. Only her group was here. "Excuse me?"

The man answered, "Sorry. My little joke. Some

acquaintances of mine have an adult drinking establishment on the other side of the base called All Guns Blazing. I figured I needed a name for this place, too. Does it work? I can change it."

Ronnie spoke up. "You could call it Grub and Stuff."

The now obvious Chef said the name a few times and smiled. "Not quite what I'm looking for. I'm sure something will leap out at me. Forgive my manners." He held out a slightly chocolate covered hand. "I'm Chef Norman, but you can call me Van."

Yana took his hand and introduced everyone. "Chef, I mean Van, can we get some snacks or something for my two friends here?"

Chef Norman eyed the two Wechselbalg boys before commenting. "If you check your tablets you will see the times for all meals as well as the fact we are open twenty-four-seven for any Wechselbalg that is hungry. Trust me when I say that I have seen some of them eat. I can make you something, or you can hit the vending machines." Van pointed to the opposite wall. Faintly lit machines lined the wall as well as Coke machines.

"They are free to use, but contain mostly healthy snacks. The Cokes aren't really good for you, but I was ordered by the Queen herself to provide them. Once we leave Earth, we may not be able to fill them, so enjoy while you can."

Maxim thought he caught a stray scent he liked and began to sniff the air. After a moment, Nestor joined him. Yana and Tina could only stare as the two larger boys started sniffing at tables and all over the dining room.

"What'cha looking for boys?" Van had a mischievous smile on his face.

"Something I have not smelled since leaving Romonavka."

PAUL and ANDERLE

Maxim looked up at Van and almost growled. "How?"

The Chef chuckled. "The Guardians all love it and say it's the best they have ever had. Believe it or not, I got the recipe from a distant aunt in my family who loved to cook. Where she got it? No idea. Want some?"

Tina and the other two humans blinked and looked around. Ronnie asked Yana, "What were they talking about?"

Maxim's cousin practically begged. "Da, Yes! Please, if the taste is anything like the smell…" He pushed past Maxim and almost leaned over the counter.

"Let me get you some bowls." The Chef stepped back into the kitchen.

"What is it you smell?" Yana almost demanded of the two Wolves.

"Heaven and home." The Chef reappeared and slid two bowls under the noses of the Wechselbalg. To Tina, it looked like some sort of soup until Yana almost grabbed Nestor's bowl to see.

"Did you want some, too? All of you?" At Yana's nod, he went back into the kitchen. Maxim and Nestor were staring at the bowls like they were figments of their imagination.

"What is it?" Ronnie peered at the bowls.

"It's Borscht. It smells like something my mama would have made." Maxim took another deep sniff and carefully took a small bite. Tears began to run down his face as he took another bite.

"Should I be upset if my food brings you to tears?" The Chef slid three more bowls out.

"Nyet. This is a taste of home. You made this?" Nestor savored another bite.

"I did. It will be added to the rotating menu and available at least once a week from now on. Is that good for you guys?"

He didn't get an answer right away. All five students were nose down in their bowls.

Yana finally came up for air and stared at Van. "How did you get it right? I have had this since leaving home, but it never tastes 'right.'"

"I listened to my clients. The secret of Siberian Borscht is the salt cabbage and amount of pepper used. Making what people like to eat is my secret."

Maxim and Nestor barely looked up from their bowls except to mumble out an "is good" before eating more.

"Is good secret. My mother…" Yana bowed her head. "The cook at my father's house made this. But, THIS is so very much better tasting. Thank you, Van. Thank you for reminding me of home and for feeding the hungry Wolves!" She patted the backs of the two Wechselbalg.

Maxim grabbed his cousin, "Come along now, Nestor. Save some for the others. You heard the man. He is open all the time; you can come back for more later." He finished as he pulled his cousin away from the counter.

"Now that their hunger is fixed, at least temporarily, let's go play some more. You said there were simulators here?" Yana raised an eyebrow at Tina.

"Yes!" Tina pointed toward the doors, "The map says they're this way."

Yana's eyes lit up just a little, "Let's go then. Pods to fly and aliens to kill!" The group marched out with a purpose.

Watching from his kitchen, Van smiled to himself, "I better place a bigger order of lamb and beets." He paused a moment. "Because, those five will eat the Empire out of house and home."

CHAPTER FIVE

B y all that is holy, can these men at least learn to write a proper sentence?" Yana stared at the paper in front of her for what seemed like the thousandth time.

"Let me see that." Tina pulled the paper over to her and stared at it. "The equations look correct as well as the notation."

She looked at the leader of her group and asked. "What has you so upset?"

"This right here! How does it connect with the equations? You see something I'm not. You have to be!" She pointed at a perfect circle in the middle of the page.

Tina took the paper back and stared at it. Suddenly, it dawned on her what Yana was talking about! "Yana, that is a ring left by someone setting a beer can on the paper. See, I have a bunch of those." She held up several papers with more circles.

Yana muttered a few half-heard phrases in Russian and threw up her hands. Again. Much of the past week had been like this.

It had started so well, too.

One week before...

Everyone was eating in the cafeteria when the school's administrators walked in.

"May we have your attention please?" The room quieted down several levels.

"Thank you. You all have had several weeks to become acclimated to both the school and the sort of schedule that we keep around here. If you check your tablets, you will notice a new tab has been added to them. Now, your assignments begin. Each of your groups will spend six weeks with one of the departments here on the station. Unless told otherwise, you will sleep and eat here at the Academy. Your instructors are focused on the future. They are strong Alpha personalities, so expect the unexpected from them. If you have any questions or concerns, my sister and I are here for you. Max will pick you up out front in an hour, so be ready. The future waits for no one." Diane and her sister turned and left the cafeteria.

"The future waits for no one? What the hell was that? That was the cheesiest thing you've said yet!" Dorene was staring at her sister.

Diane blushed, "Sorry? It was all I could think of on the fly."

"What about all the speeches you had ME write for you? Did you forget all of them?" Dorene couldn't believe her sister. She just shook her head.

"Pretty much, yeah." Diane waved her hands. "It got the point across. We have an hour before Max gets here with the train, did you want to stay and say 'hi' to him?"

"To Max? Are you crazy? You know as well as I do that Running Wolf has a thing for him! That would be worse than pinching John again." Dorene shuddered. "She's a doctor and has lots of sharp, pointy things. Besides, she knows where we sleep."

Dorene looked sideways at her sister, "You're just trying to get me killed."

Diane smirked, "It gets boring around here. I have to find humor somewhere."

Dorene blew out a breath. "I'll give you humor! Come on, let's get out of the way before we get trampled."

The cafeteria doors burst open, and students streamed out heading in multiple directions at once. They acknowledged the bickering sisters, but had already witnessed their behavior before.

Nothing new here, move along, move along.

Thirty teenagers might not sound like a lot, but when they are charging at you all at once, it can seem that way. Both of the D's froze in their tracks and watched as the stream of kids parted in the middle and went around them.

"That was cool! Let's do it again." Dorene looked at her sister with wide eyes.

"Let's not and say we did." The two sisters continued walking, "Did you notify the departments they were getting interns today?" Diane looked sternly at her sister.

"No. I thought that was your job as Administrator." Dorene replied in a snarky voice.

"I thought we agreed… Dorene, you're killing me here.

ALPHA CLASS

We have a bunch of calls to make and in a hurry, too!" The twins scurried off to notify extremely busy people they were about to be invaded.

Whether they liked it or not.

"Yana, what should we take with us?" Ronnie looked up at the older girl.

"The stuff they issued us for sure. This says we have Team BMW as our first class. Why are we being taught by car makers?" Yana held up her tablet.

Tina spoke up, "BMW? For real? That's awesome! Marcus himself will teach us. Yana, you will love it! Team BMW is the one that made the pods and helped design this place. The guys on that team are so cool!" Tina was beside herself.

"This Marcus, he is the one who introduced you to space? That Marcus?" Maxim stared down at the smaller girl.

"Yes. He used to work for NASA, Space-X, and a few of the others. He's brilliant!"

Nestor piped in, "Maybe this won't be so boring after all."

"It shouldn't be, Nestor. Marcus is a fun guy. But then, so are William and Bobcat." Tina really was excited. She had always wanted to work with Marcus. He had taught her so much about orbital mechanics and trajectory targeting when she was younger.

"This Bobcat is Were? He comes from China?" Maxim almost growled the words.

"No, no Maxim. It's just his nickname, that's all." Tina cocked her head to one side as she searched her memory.

"I think his real name is William something. I can't remember his last name. Everyone just calls him Bobcat, even the Queen."

The large Were nodded his head. "Is good."

"Do any of you need clothes or anything? The train should be here soon." Yana looked at all of them.

None of the others in the group moved. They all looked at the tall blond girl attentively. This was one group that was actually a unit, leader and all. Their bond had developed early and was holding so far.

"Good. We should go outside, then." Yana led her small team out the large double doors into the main corridor of the Asteroid base. Dozens of pathways like this zigzagged through the base. An invader would be hard pressed to discover the proper way around without a map. Physical maps didn't exist and were not posted. Why, when you had only to ask aloud, and the base's E.I. would answer your question?

The people-mover train looked to be the same one as before with Max, the school's maintenance supervisor, as the driver. Several of the other groups slowly made their way outside to join Team Alpha standing by the main doors. Many of the other teens carried notebooks and excessive clothing items.

"Should I have brought a coat, too?" Ronnie looked over at Yana.

"Only if you wish one. It seems comfortable in here now. There is no 'outside' to go to, so it's up to you."

Ronnie nodded. "One of my favorite authors calls that 'Earth think.' We should adopt it. We don't belong down there anymore, do we?"

"No, Ron. We don't." Tina tapped her chin with a finger, before continuing. "'Earth think,' sounds like a good way to explain the differences. Tell me about your favorite authors later. I like to read, too." Ron got the shivers when she smiled at him.

"You kids ready to go?" Max was now standing in front of the train.

"Uh, guys? Did you see this?" William held up his tablet for the others. They were hard at work trying to configure one of the Pods so it could hold more than two people. They had made a five-person Pod work, but the boss said she wanted more.

"What is it?" Marcus had his head down and was peering at a notation on the holographic table.

William continued, "Did you forget that today was the first day of class?"

"Hmm, class? What class would that be?" Marcus tried to fine tune the virtual engines for the Pod. Four just wasn't cutting it. Maybe six?

"The Academy class that will be showing up in about a half hour. Five kids that you are supposed to teach. Remember now?" he asked, without much patience.

"What? Is that today?" Marcus rose up with a jerk. "How many did you say?"

William hit a button on his tablet and stared at it for a moment. "This says five. But it's for six weeks."

"Six weeks? That can't be right. Let me see that." Marcus reached for the tablet, but William pulled it back.

"Uh, uh. The last time you took mine, it got left behind on the moon! Use your own."

"Fine." Marcus jerked out his tablet and called up the

information. "No. We don't have time for this today. Tell them to come back later."

Bobcat opened a beer and set it on the table. "It doesn't work that way, and you know it. Don't worry I have just the thing to keep them busy and out of our way."

"What?" asked Marcus.

"I've got this. Don't worry about it." Bobcat smiled to the two of them.

This would kill two birds with one stone.

The ride on the train was, as always, one of the best parts of the trip. Every day, the engineers made functional and other safety improvements to the station. Updates on construction were posted often, and everyone was excited to hear they might have a virtual sun inside the base before long.

"We're almost there, guys!" Tina was excited to see her friends again.

"I hope this is everything you say it will be, Tina. These guys sound a bit boring." Maxim had pulled a knife from somewhere and was cleaning his nails, as he spoke.

"It is, I promise. It's not just them. They have a ton of engineers and scientists backing them up. Look at this train. They had a hand in creating it, too." The others looked down at their feet for a moment. The magnetic propulsion train was state-of-the-art.

Ronnie looked around the car and pulled up the video map on his tablet. They had passed through the main part of the asteroid, stopping numerous times to drop off groups of kids. According to the map, only the engineering and BMW areas were left. Even now he could feel the train starting to slow down.

"This must be the Engineering area." Ronnie peered out of the window of the car. "It looks like Delta team gets to work with them this session."

"Engineering would be cool. My mom said they are building the interior of the base as well as working in the shipyard."

"Do they fly around in space with jetpacks?" Nestor peered out of the window, too.

Tina looked at him funny. "I don't know. They might. We will find out in six weeks, according to the schedule. So, unless Delta tells us…"

"Cool." The older boy sat back down with a smile to find the others watching him. "I read about it in a comic book."

They all felt a slight movement as the train resumed motion. Their stop was next!

"Tina, have you been where we are going?"

"I have, but not for several months. I've known Marcus for years. William and Bobcat are like brothers from another mother the way they act. When we lived on the old Space Station, I saw them almost every day. But since we moved here, I've been busy with school and helping to take care of the littles."

"You worked in the nursery?" Yana looked over at her friend.

"Yep. In the beginning, they needed lots of help. Since the Queen opened us up to immigration, there are plenty of certified day care people now for the center."

"Does it worry you that the wrong sort of individuals might get up here? I mean, spies are everywhere in Russia. What keeps them from coming up here, too?" Nestor stared at Tina.

She answered, "Nestor, I know you would be able to sniff out anything with that nose of yours, right? The Queen has people who do the same sort of thing with other senses. We are safe here."

Yana put her hand on Nestor's arm. "If I can trust these people, you can, too. You know what the Cheka would do to me."

Tina looked puzzled, "You keep mentioning the Cheka, Yana. Who are they?"

Yana made a spitting noise. "They are Russian secret police. They were known as KGB many years ago, and NVA now. Evil, evil men. They have hunted my family for almost a hundred years. Romanovka was our last refuge. We were moved so many times I lost count. My mother was not so lucky as I."

"Why? Why hunt you down? You're just a kid like us," she asked.

"Politics, hatred, status maybe? Hunt down the unreachable. My family has a claim to the throne of Russia. Is a moot point now. Part of something else. Something better. As you say, that is Earth think now." Yana stared out the window.

Tina laid her hand on her friend's arm. "I'm sorry, Yana. Sorry about your mother. Does that make you a princess?"

Maxim began to laugh. "She could be a queen if she wanted to, even we know that. That option is gone now."

Yana spoke, "He's right about that option being gone now. We abdicated and swore fealty to a new Queen, a more powerful one. Earth and Russia are no longer my destiny."

The train began to slow down again. "This looks like our stop. Time to go to school."

CHAPTER SIX

"Are you sure this is the place?" Ronnie looked at the simple door cut into the rock wall. He had been outside of All Guns Blazing, it was garish and loud. This was just a door without any signs or names on it.

Tina shrugged, "I've been here before. Bobcat calls this his lair, so I guess they want it to be secret?"

The five kids stood outside of an unassuming plain metal door. Max had dropped them off telling them to "go on in."

"Do we just go in?" Yana looked at Tina. She claimed to have been here before.

"Sure. Come on." Tina opened the door and stepped inside. The door opened to a smallish room that only contained another door and a scanner station. It was blinking on and off. The device was brand new to Tina's eyes, and she didn't know what to do now.

"Problems?"

"Sorry, Yana. That wasn't here last time. Maybe they have a doorbell?" None of them could see a button.

Nestor called out to the E.I., "Meredith? Can you tell the BMW team we are here?" Everyone turned to stare at him.

"Certainly, Nestor. Thank you for asking."

Seeing the looks, he held out his hands in supplication. "What? You are the ones that said the E.I. knows everything."

"We did, but we didn't think you were listening." Tina grinned at the boy.

A loud BOOM echoed through the door causing everyone to jump just a bit. The scanner lights changed from red to green as the opposite door opened.

"Hello, Tina. Who are your friends?" A man in what looked like military fatigues stepped into the room.

"Hi, Bobcat! This is my new team from the Academy," she pointed to everyone as she introduced them, "Yana, Ronnie, Nestor, and Maxim."

Bobcat nodded to all the new interns and smiled. "We aren't quite ready for you inside at the moment. Marcus is working on a delicate systems drawing that requires his constant attention. However, I have a project you can get started on that should make the time pass rather quickly."

Waving his hand over the scanner causing the door to open.

Peering at the flashing lights, Ronnie looked sharply at Bobcat. "Biometric?"

Bobcat shook his head, "Not anymore. We had a few problems with unannounced visitors, and some of the enhanced folk don't have fingerprints anymore. The scanners work on both DNA and computer monitoring. Meredith double checks all entrants, just in case. All of you have had your DNA entered into the system as part of your enrollment testing. Not every system door will open to you, but as you progress in your education that will be updated, too." He led them through the large door.

The door led to a 'T' intersection of unmarked doors and hallways, he pointed down one. "Down there is the access to 'All Guns Blazing,' our bar. You are all underage, so that door won't open for you. Back the other way, are the workshops and our manufacturing area. We will go that way later, but for now, you will be working in the office section."

The offices were a quartet of doors along one wall. On the other wall was a small kitchenette complete with Alcoholic vending machines. "Those are off-limits, too. My office is down there at the end. William and Marcus have these offices." Bobcat pointed to the doors in the middle.

He led them to the last door. As it opened the door, he spoke. "This is the project I have for you."

File cabinets lined one wall as well as three large piles of boxes. A table with chairs stood in the middle of the room. Scanners and computer input devices were set up and looked ready to use.

"The job I have for you is simple. Input the files and contents of the boxes into the system. Super easy."

Yana looked at the boxes, there must have been over thirty of them. "All of these?"

Bobcat looked around, "Sure. This is all stuff from before we came up here and went entirely digital. Research notes, a few blueprints and sketches, tech diagrams, and all the mathematical equations. We couldn't safely leave it at any of the bases, but haven't transferred it yet. It should keep you busy. Have fun." He left contact information and directions to the bathroom facilities.

Yana turned to stare at Tina who looked a bit down and

mumbled, "That was a bit uncool of him."

Yana nodded, "You think so? We might as well see what we need to do. Maxim, can you bring one of those boxes over here?" The large Were grabbed a box like it weighed nothing and set it on the table.

It may have been a file box, but it was filled to the brim with loose paper. Ronnie peered into the box. "Are all of them like this? This could take forever!"

"He did say they were busy in the labs. It's just busy work." Frustrated, Tina grabbed a handful and began to sort it.

Nestor shook his head. "They should be more prepared for students. It's school after all."

"Marcus can be a little scatterbrained when he's working. The three of them have been at the forefront of TQB technical developments. The Queen trusts them. We should, too." Tina looked at her friends.

"If you say so." Ronnie sat down at one of the terminals, "I trust you, Tina."

The rest of the day was spent pouring over the many notes and diagrams. One box was what appeared to be bets and payoffs.

"Should we even record this stuff?" Ronnie held up a sheaf of papers, "It looks like the results of betting who would grab a hot piece of metal first."

"They like both jokes and betting here. Set it aside; we can ask Bobcat about it." Tina took the papers and glanced at them with an audible sigh.

"What does electrogravitic propulsion mean? Is it the properties that make the Pods go?" Maxim held up a sheet of paper.

"Ooo, that may be some of the original research work.

What else does it say?" Tina tried to look at the paper he was holding.

"Something about 'Project Winterhaven' and using electrostatic energy sources coupled with a form of gravitic energy to produce lift in saucer-shaped craft," he answered. "Did this come from TOM?"

Ronnie spoke as he looked at his own handful of papers, "Project Winterhaven is a catch phrase for secret projects the US Government did in the 1950s using Tesla technology along with some stuff stolen from the Russians to build their own version of flying saucers. Or at least according to some groups on the internet."

He looked up to see everyone staring at him. "What? Secret societies and aliens are sort of a hobby of mine, sorry."

"Don't be sorry, Ron. It's a good hobby to have. We are in space after all, and The Queen knows an alien." Yana smiled at him.

"Good work, Ron." Tina beamed at him which gave him goosebumps all over. It was only later that he realized they all called him Ron instead of Ronnie.

"Eight engine points along with an extra generator is what we need to make the ten-passenger pod function the same as the others. TOM agrees that more power is better than less. What do you two think?" Marcus looked up from his calculations at the holo table.

"Uh, what did you say?" William was staring at his tablet making notes on a piece of paper.

"What are you doing?" Marcus pointed to the paper.

"Making notes. Why?"

PAUL AND ANDERLE

"Do it on the tablet, please. We already have an entire room filled with hard copy research. Don't make more of it! What do you think of the Pod?" Marcus pointed toward the hologram.

"I like it. According to my figures," William held up the paper. "We should be able to make the shell here in the fabrication shop. It's four times as big, but we can save material here, here, and here by using those new composites they cooked up by accident in Jean's area. It will save on weight, too."

"Why worry about that? The extra engines we are placing will lift a chunk of metal the size of… of… a jumbo jet."

"Call it material cost then. You forget, I'm used to dealing with cheapskates like Bobcat." William pointed with his thumb toward the man in question.

Bobcat looked up from his own work, "Hey! I resemble that remark."

Marcus raised his eyebrows and laughed. "Forget about cost. These are for the Queen. Those composites look good, and we can use them for some of the other projects. What were they making that created them?" Marcus squinted at William's tablet over his shoulder.

"Jean wouldn't say. Some sort of armor, I think. We would have to test it, but that might be good for re-plating the older spacecraft."

"Pass that off to the captains and shipbuilding. We don't need another project dumped on us. Say, what happened to those kids?" Marcus looked between his two brothers-in-arms.

Bobcat jerked a thumb over his shoulder, "I put them to work in the file room," he replied.

Marcus stared for a moment, "Doing what? Some of that is necessary research."

Bobcat looked up, "They are cataloging it, and doing

57

some data entry. It's a good way to get it done and clear that room out at the same time. We could use the space."

"For what? We can always hollow out another room." Marcus waved at the walls.

"I ordered an industrial walk-in cooler for libation storage." William gave Bobcat a smile and the two fist-bumped.

Marcus shook his head, "You two. Fine. Whatever, it's your area. Did you look at my calculations?"

"It makes me wonder if ADAM dug up some of that for them. Some of it was pretty far out there."

"We could ask him if you like. If it's a secret, they just won't tell us." Tina stopped and looked over at Ron.

"Hey, move along lovebirds; you can talk over dinner. I'm hungry." Maxim pushed his way past the now blushing duo.

"You two are cute. You know that, right?" Yana squeezed past them.

"We're just friends," Ron yelled after her.

Nestor picked Ron up and moved him rather than squeeze past, "Sure you are. The pheromones you are putting off tells me different."

Still blushing, Tina glanced at Ron. His face looked surprised as his classmate set him down.

"Come on, let's go eat something," Tina said.

CHAPTER SEVEN

Do we have to go back today? I mean the boxes are all done. Those filing cabinets scare me."

"Ron, I'm sure they haven't forgotten about us. I mean they keep refilling the vending machines. Right?" Even Tina was looking a bit down in the dumps as she talked.

Yana glanced down at her tvorog and smetana. The yogurt dish was starting to get a bit boring, and she thought that switching to another option might be in order. Chef Norman just had to be a secret magician. He was able to come up with so many tastes of home. Even the non-Russian kids were enjoying the meals. Except for the caviar and liver dishes. Only the Weres enjoyed those. Too strong of a taste for her. "We should either ask or report them somehow. It only makes sense. We are learning nothing that will help us later."

"Yana, I'm learning about electrogravitic engines and magnetic fields. Some of that research could only have come from Tesla's research. I wonder where they found it?" Ron commented.

"Ron, only you like that stuff. Even Tina's eyes are starting to cross. Yana's right. We need to report to someone about it." Maxim stood up from the breakfast table.

"Whoa, there big fellow! Why don't you sit back down and tell me all about it?" Maxim felt a strong but firm hand on his back.

Dorene sat down and stared at everyone. "What is this all about? Is Marcus too hard on you?"

"Uh, we haven't seen him yet. We are working to digitize old files."

"All week? Has no one taught you anything? Who have you been talking to? Tell me right now." The smallish woman now had a fiery gleam in her eye.

"Miss Dorene, we don't want to cause trouble." Surprised by the sudden change in the little woman, Tina tried to pull back.

"Dear, you are here to learn, not be someone's secretary. We have others that can do that sort of thing. Now. Who did it, Bobcat or William?"

"It was Bobcat. He assigned us the task after telling us that Marcus was too busy to see us." Maxim almost cringed when he said it. Waiting for the blow, he leaned back in his chair.

"I see. Well, you kids finish your breakfast. I will fix this. Do not leave until I tell you. Understood?" Five heads nodded yes as the little woman stormed out of the room.

"Did I say the wrong thing?" Maxim worriedly looked at Tina who knew those involved better than he did.

"No, you didn't. I think she will take care of it without going to the Queen. Not a good time to be named Bobcat right now."

PAUL AND ANDERLE

⚜ ⚜ ⚜

The brains behind BMW were just starting their day in the main workshop when doom arrived.

"I had a brilliant idea last night. We have already talked about using that new composite to beef up the armor on the outside of ships. But what if we use it internally, too?"

"By internally, what do you mean?" Marcus cocked his head and stared at Bobcat.

"Just the bulkheads and support structures. We beefed those up during the refit, but with this new stuff, we could ensure that a penetrator doesn't breach the security doors and make it into the superstructure of a ship. Here, let me show you." He was just turning on the holo-table when they all heard the outer door open with a slam.

"Bobcat, get your ass out here right now!" The voice was female and furious.

"Who is that?" Bobcat looked at his two friends who were looking at him and called out to the E.I. "Meredith, who is in the outer room?" Bobcat looked up at the ceiling.

The E.I. intelligence that ran the Asteroid knew all and heard all. "The person in the outer room is Dorene, one of the Academy administrators. Her twin sister Diane is en route to your location also."

"Crap!" Bobcat looked around wildly as if searching for a place to hide.

"What is going on? Wait? The Academy. I'm supposed to teach a class or something there, aren't I?" Marcus turned toward William.

"Don't look at me." The large man pointed at his friend who was now staring at a shipping container full of parts. "He said he took care of it."

ALPHA CLASS

Marcus's head looked over to Bobcat, "What did you do, Bill?"

Bobcat winced. When Marcus used his real name, he knew he had probably stepped into something. "The students showed up last week, and you said you didn't have time for them. I put them to work clearing out the paperwork storage area. They have been scanning and doing data entry."

"We are supposed to teach them. That is the reason for the school after all. You should have told me." He looked up. "Meredith Reynolds, please let the lady in."

A short, extremely pissed off, redheaded woman stormed into the lab completely ignoring both Marcus and William. "I've got a bone to pick with you, mister!" She marched right up to Bobcat and began poking him in the chest with her finger.

"What." Poke. "Gives." Poke. "You." Poke. "The right to pigeonhole those kids and make them your own personal paperwork slaves?" Poke.

"I didn't…" Bobcat started to defend himself.

"What?" Poke. "Who put them to work without teaching them anything?" Poke.

"But I…" Poke.

"You gave them food and water? Like good little slaves?" Poke.

Bobcat grabbed her hand to stop the next round. He held up his other hand. "Whoa! Look, I gave them some busy work when Marcus said he was too busy to teach. They were doing such a good job, I left them in there." He smiled at her and tried for a sad puppy dog look.

Dorene wasn't buying it. She yanked her hand out of his and spun on Marcus. "You!"

Marcus held his tablet up in front of his stomach, "What?"

He looked at his best friend who had just thrown him under the bus and shook his head.

"You knew the kids were coming. The Academy was your idea, remember? You didn't bother to teach them, so you let Bozo over here make them sort papers for a week?"

"Hey, my name is Bobcat." Dorene ignored him completely. She continued to focus on Marcus.

"So? Do you have anything different to say?"

"Uh, no? I didn't know about the fact they were even here. I just found out this morning."

She snorted. "A likely story. Here is what is going to happen." She looked at all of them, including William this time.

"You and Bozo here are going to teach them something. These kids are the future of our Empire! They came to the Academy to learn. You will teach them, or I'm coming back! Do you hear the words coming out of my mouth?"

All three men could only nod their heads, yes.

"Good. Now, what are the plans for today? They better be good ones too." She folded her arms in front of her and glared at all three of them.

"Uh, we could take them out in a Pod and … uh." Bobcat looked back at William mouthing 'help me' to him.

"Yeah, we can take the Pods and teach them about maneuvers and show them how to pilot…"

"Wrong! We have a piloting class for that over in piloting. Bozo, sit down. You, too, William." She looked back at Marcus.

"What you got, smart stuff?" she asked the scientist.

Marcus looked to his friends for help, but they were trying to hide from the scary woman. "We are dismantling the moon base we established and cleaning up all the tech scattered around. No sense in leaving it for NASA to find. The students can help sort and pack up. We still have living quarters down there along with supplies. Since they aren't adults, they will only work eight hours..." Dorene shook her head at him.

"Six hours..." Another shake.

"Four hours?" She gave him a big smile. "Four hours on the project, the rest of the time can be lectures and maybe some show-and-tell. NASA and the Soviets, as well as the Chinese, left a bunch of junk up there. We are cleaning and recycling all of it," Marcus informed her.

"Good plan, boys. I will outfit the kids for a week of travel and study. Make sure you have skinsuits for all five as well as backups. Nice chatting with you... You can go back to work now." Dorene did a smart about-face and exited the room, leaving the three stunned men behind.

"I blame you for this." Marcus looked at Bobcat who was rubbing his chest and stomach.

"Me? Why? That woman is all your doing. Remember, you created the Academy."

"That may be, but you could have given me some warning they were coming, rather than bet with William about it." He began to chuckle, "Bozo."

"She did get you there, Bobcat." William began to laugh.

Dorene ran into her sister halfway to the Academy. "Did you fix it?"

"Of course I did."

"Are they still alive? Or do I need to go in, too?" Diane looked past Dorene toward the BMW area.

"They are fine. We need to get the kids packed, they're

headed to the moon to help break the base down."

"Ooh, that should be fun! They will enjoy that." Diane reversed course and followed her sister.

"They will need a week's worth of stuff, as well as skin-suits. I told them to include backups, or I was going back. I may have scared them just a bit."

"Knowing you, you scared them a lot. I remember what happened at the last family reunion."

Dorene smiled at the memory of that incident. "It wasn't entirely my fault that time. That cop should have watched where he walked."

Snorting Diane chuckled. "You had him so flustered, he walked right off the edge of the pool! Admit it, you can be scary."

"I have no idea what you are saying." The two continued to bicker as they entered the main hall of the school.

The two administrators found Team Alpha upstairs in the simulation room.

"…go Ron. You've almost got her!" Tina stood behind the simulator, cheering on her friend.

"Hurry, Yana! He is almost here."

Gritting her teeth, Yana cursed in Russian. "Stop yelling at me, Maxim!" The Sim-Pod she was operating swerved to the left, then suddenly rolled to the right, directly into an Immelmann Turn maneuver.

"Whoa, that was cool!" Ron said as he looked all around for her Pod.

Yana, her Pod now above and behind Ron, came screaming down and scored on him.

"You have GOT to teach me that!" Ron yelled, as his cockpit went red and his controls froze.

"I will, Ron. I will. Wait until we pilot for real." She got out of the Pod and walked over to pat the smaller boy on the back.

"Tina, how did you do against Nestor?" Yana asked.

"He smoked me as usual. Yana, he is getting really good."

Yana's eyes lit up, "Good. We will have our own squadron someday. Take the fight to the enemy."

There was a light knock on the door which caused even the Wechselbalg kids to jump. They didn't smell or hear the women come down the hall.

Diane and Dorene stepped in, "Sorry. This room is shielded and soundproofed as well as having special climate controls. Those Pod sims are state-of-the-art when it comes to TQB tech, and they have special needs. I have your new assignments. The gentlemen at BMW are taking the five of you down to the Moonbase. Expect to stay at least a week." Dorene informed them.

"The Moon? I thought the base down there was already closed?" Tina looked at the twin Admins.

"Not yet. They want you to help them with that. You will be issued the new skinsuits along with all your survival gear. Marcus, William, and Boz... I mean Bobcat will go with you. For four hours each day, you will help them recycle and break things down. This is a golden chance to get your space legs and a feel for the new suits. Go pack. Take light outfits and the long underwear you were all issued."

"Why long underwear?" Tina asked.

"It is what you'll wear under your skinsuit. Your body needs the extra layer of protection. It's not traditional underwear, it's made of a special material. You were all issued those and told to leave it in the wrapper." Diane waved them toward the doors. "Move it!" Once they were out of the room, she muttered, "Kids."

PAUL AND ANDERLE

Dorene chuckled at her sister.

Ron hurried to keep up with his classmates. He was beside himself with excitement. The Moon! One of his hobbies was conspiracy theories and their ties to space exploration. It didn't matter to him that he was already in space or that Aliens existed. The Moon was the goal of most space fanatics down on Earth, and he was actually going there!

CHAPTER EIGHT

This is so cool!" Ron had said the same thing at least twenty times so far.

Nestor could only roll his eyes. "Ron, you know we have been in space for months now, right?"

"I know that, Nestor. But space isn't the Moon! It's the first celestial body that man walked on, and we get to do it, too!"

Nestor covered his own mouth so as not to respond. Or he at least covered where his mouth should be. The new skin-suits were exactly as advertised. Skin tight. The instantaneous radio communication was pretty cool as well.

Both boys were riding with William in one of the two, experimental, five-passenger Pods they had created. The Queen had told them to make bigger ones, so these were the only mid-sized Pods in existence.

"Hey, William, why are we going around the Mare

Crisium? I thought the Sea of Tranquility was over there?" Ron pointed in another direction.

William smiled, "You're better than a map book, Ron. Do you know all the craters?"

"Most of them. Or at least those related to NASA missions." Ron agreed.

"Well, something that NASA didn't tell you, the area around the Mare Crisium has some sort of electromagnetic field around it. Our etheric sensors tripped it after we lost a couple of probes. The geologists say it may be a rare magnetic mineral. We were about to dig it up to see, but BA, I mean the Queen, said wait. Earth has been getting pissy about us up here, and strip mining the moon would really irritate them. So, we go around. Less chance of damaging the Pod that way."

"I wonder if NASA knows about it?" Ron asked.

William glanced at Ron and smiled. "You can ask Marcus that if you like. He might know. We're coming up on the base ahead. It's in the Sinus Medii Mare if you are trying to locate it."

Ahead of the Pod was a rocky area with large rock formations. Domed buildings could be seen sticking up here and there among large shipping containers.

Ron's eyes went wide, "Wow, this is huge!"

The Pod zipped down for a landing as the central dome opened up like a clamshell to receive it. William expertly flew the Pod down and landed next to the other five-person Pod. Several prototype three-person Pods lined the interior wall.

William called back to his group, "Wait for the dome to close. The suits will protect you, but without gravity, you will bounce easily and find yourself missing things and landing badly. Here on the Moon, unless you are in the base, you have to wear special gravity boots. We have enough for all of you, so don't worry about not getting a pair."

The dome above them silently closed, and a faint sucking noise was heard. The control panel in the Pod made a loud *ding* sound.

"That's the signal for atmosphere. Time to go boys." The Pod opened at William's touch. The three of them stepped out onto the hangar deck.

"It's about time you got here, pokey." Bobcat stepped over from the wall he was leaning on.

William shrugged, "I took the long way to show the kids more of the Moon. Everything OK inside?"

"Yup. They left the supplies alone and only took the scientific equipment as planned. We still have to send the fabricators back up, but they should fit in the containers. It's how we got them here after all." Bobcat visually checked the Pod, out of habit, looking for damage.

"Good. What does Marcus think our schedule should be?" William pulled out the bags belonging to the two boys and threw them at them.

"He thinks we should strip the place first. Send out the containers and then pound the domes with pucks. Explosive charges might be easier."

"You know, Jean has interns like we do. She might like to use them as target practice." William stared at the dome overhead.

Bobcat smirked, "The domes, not the kids, right?"

"What?" William thought about what he said. "Yeah, sorry. Off in la la land, apparently. The domes not the kids. Ha! That's pretty funny. Let's get everyone settled in, and then we can get started."

Bobcat led them through a small tunnel to the adjoining dome.

PAUL AND ANDERLE

Marcus pointed, "That pile is Chinese junk we picked up the last time we were here. It's a couple of probes and their Change 2 capsule which crashed when William gave it a good nudge with the Pod."

In front of Marcus was a small unit that looked like it came off a cement mixer. One side was crushed, but you could still see the blue triangle of the CNSA.

William gave Marcus a small wave as he passed by him. Marcus then explained, "Our goal up here was two-fold. We wanted to establish a presence here initially, and test some of our technology. Now that we are leaving, it is vital that no country on Earth gains any sort of technological boost from our equipment here. So, we are gathering it all up. Including the junk others have left as well. My former employers aren't very happy about it, and neither are the Russians."

"Sir? Why would they be worried now? It's just junk, right?" Nestor pointed to the Chinese capsule pile.

"That one is now. But when we knocked it out of orbit, it was still functional and being used to spy on us. Take that piece over there." He pointed to what looked a bit like a baby carriage with a solar panel on it.

"Wow! A Lunokhod rover! Is that number one or two?" Ron stepped over to it and peered inside.

"Very good, Ron. That is number one. It and its brother have been deactivated, but they were still operating and sending signals out even after being sent up here in the early 1970s. Both the owner and the Russian Government have protested about it." Marcus informed the group.

"Uh, isn't the owner the Government? I don't understand." Maxim stepped over and tried lifting the little robotic rover.

"Funny story, Ron might know more than I since he's a

fan. A private individual bought number two from the Russians in a public auction, making him the only private citizen to have something up here. Until we got here, that is."

"How much did he pay for this thing?"

Ron jumped in. "He paid $68,000 dollars. That's like four million Rubles."

"For this? And he had to leave it up here?" Maxim gave it a kick.

"It was pretty advanced for its time. Even NASA would have been hard pressed to equal it. They actually sent it up with radioactive material inside. We have since removed the polonium-210 it contained." Maxim jumped back from the machine.

"Are the Lunar Rovers from Apollo fifteen, sixteen, and seventeen here, too?" Ron looked around.

"Outside. They still work. The science crew that was working here souped them up and replaced the batteries and fragile bumpers. They even took out the hard to steer controls and put in an actual steering wheel. Bobcat may have had something to do with that. He called them 'dune buggies' instead of rovers." Marcus grinned at the memory.

Marcus then pointed to the large pile behind him. "The rest of this stuff has NASA written all over it. Probes, sensor packages, and spy satellites. We even found some off-the-books stuff."

"Like Apollo twenty?" Ron looked up from his investigation of a NASA probe.

"That one is definitely a hoax, but we found a few items that didn't come with any of the documented missions. So, who knows." He looked at Ron. "You, young man, need to have a conversation with me someday about spacecraft and NASA."

PAUL AND ANDERLE

Yana was starting to look like she was sleeping. It was exciting, and all, but spacecraft history was boring to her.

"Let's go find the living quarters and get you set up. We won't start work until tomorrow anyway."

"Ron, how did you get into NASA and conspiracies?" Maxim softly asked him. The boys were on one end of the sleeping chamber, the girls the other.

"Dad is a big shot computer programmer. He's one of the ones that helped to create ADAM. We first lived in Colorado at the TQB base there. After my school class had been kidnapped, I started looking into mysterious happenings around the country. Most were obviously Forsaken or Wechselbalg, once I knew they existed. So, I began looking into space. We knew that at least one alien existed, why not more? The space agencies all deny it, but ultimately that is what they search for, aliens."

"And this sort of information is just available on the Internet?" Maxim rolled over and stared at the younger boy.

"Sure. As one of my favorite movies says. You can't stop the signal. Once it's on the Internet, it cannot be removed completely. Dad says even ADAM has trouble taking stuff down for the Queen."

"Interesting. When we get back, can you show me some of how you search?"

"Sure, Maxim. I can do that." Ron closed his eyes. It had been a long day.

"What are you looking for?" Nestor whispered into the room. Maxim's sharp ears caught it anyway.

"Father. Surely there is some sign or report I can read. I

73

want to be able to mourn him."

"I understand, Cousin."

At the other end of the room, Yana and Tina sat on their beds. "What is your opinion of conspiracy theory?"

Tina cocked her head to one side and smiled. "Ron gets a bit extreme for me. There is some truth in it, though. The UnknownWorld does exist, as well as aliens after all. Many of the Governments of the world have proven they can't be trusted either. My mom has told me as much, too. Much of what is out there on the internet is just crazy, though."

Yana nodded. "Back in Russia, it is hard to know what to believe. The state… well, the state controls everything. You have to believe what they say. Freedom is a luxury, even without the Soviets."

"You can trust us, Yana. The Queen will protect you."

"That, I am believing. How do you like the Moon?" Yana smiled at Tina.

"It's big and open. Too bad there isn't any air. It would be fun to explore a bit."

"We could take one of those rover things and look around. Marcus might let us."

"I will ask later if you like. Marcus likes me." Tina laughed. "I was the first kid in space because of him."

"Was that fun?" Yana sometimes found it hard to believe others had fun adventures.

"It was crazy fun. Mom just about killed him, though. He didn't say 'outer space' when she asked where he was taking me. For me, though, it was a blast. We raced a meteor and buzzed the Moon. Fun." Tina smiled as she remembered the experience.

"It sounds like it. We better get some rest then. Goodnight."

PAUL AND ANDERLE

Breakfast was protein shakes and survival biscuits. Maxim was missing the school cafeteria already.

"Today, we are packing up the manufacturing plant, as well as the machine shop. Gravity in those areas has been set low, so everything will be drastically lighter. Be sure to watch your teammates carefully. Having a half-ton of machinery moved in your direction can be deadly due to mass, so be careful. Later, after lunch, Marcus has a mathematics class on basic orbital mechanics. Should be fun." Bobcat smiled at the looks on their faces.

Math and kids.

"Are we having fun yet?" Maxim grunted as his cousin tossed him a computer module.

"This is a workout, not fun! Why did they bring all of this here if they weren't leaving it?" Nestor asked.

Bobcat answered, "William might have mentioned to you the magnetic anomaly to the North of us? Well, we think it has a high concentration of iron and other ferrous material. The initial plan was to dig and mine it out for use on the first space stations. Then the UN started whining, and the US, Russia, and China joined them in making waves. Bethany Anne then moved the mining to the asteroid belt. Farther away and less prying eyes out there. We had everything all set up to start when the plan was canceled. It's only now that we have the time to pick it back up for storage. A few of the techs have been down here to tweak the sensors, but it's been pretty much just us. NASA has been raising holy hell about the loss of sensors and cameras they have denied even having up here. It's pretty funny."

"Oh. I wondered. Much of this looks new." Maxim said, setting another module inside the shipping container.

"It is. We will store everything, and when we get on the other side of the gate, we'll pull it back out. This way it's all in one place and ready." Bobcat logged each item they put away.

"What about all the space junk in the other dome?" Ron dragged a large spool of wire over to the container.

"That, we are throwing into one of the other containers. Lots of salvage there. We can always use high-end composites and lightweight materials. Many of the other departments have one project or another that needs materials."

"What about the technology?" Yana looked up from the system she was disconnecting.

"What about it? This stuff is just junk compared to what we have up in the Meredith Reynolds."

He pointed up to space. "This stuff is just cluttering up the moon, so we're disposing of it. We did leave the flags and the base of Apollo eleven in place. The Queen instructed us to put up a very nice monument commemorating the landing on the moon and those that lost their lives getting here. We tried very hard to not disturb any of Neil Armstrong or Buzz Aldrin's footsteps. Trust me when I say, moving NASA's junk without making a mess is a chore, even with the magnetic beam."

A low chime sounded, and Bobcat looked around. "Lecture time. Have a good time and try not to fall asleep. Marcus can get on a roll and forget you're not as interested in what he is teaching as he is."

CHAPTER NINE

"Not another lecture. I'm not sure my brain can take another one!" Maxim mockingly clutched his head causing the girls to laugh.

"He's not all that bad. His theory on gravitational anomalies is brilliant." Tina tried to defend her friend.

Maxim stared at Tina for a moment, "That may be true, but did we have to hear all of it? He lost me at vertical deflection, physical geodesy, and gravimetry. Have you asked him about the rovers yet?"

Tina bit the inside of her cheek, "I'll ask today. I promise."

Marcus walked into the room and stared at the five kids. "So, for today's lecture, I thought we would continue on the science of Gravimetric analysis and how it relates to what we do with our current technology. If you remember from yesterday's session gravimetric analysis is what we use…"

"Marcus, Sir?" Yana raised her hand.

Marcus stopped talking and looked at the tall Russian girl. "Yes, Yana?"

"Will we be using any of these principles in our work on the base or during operations?" she asked.

"Not normally. We use this form of science to speculate on how one body differs from another."

"So, it's not something we need to know for any operation then?" Yana smiled to herself.

"Hmm, you have a point, Miss Konstantinovich. How about we discuss regolith then, instead?"

Nestor stood. "Sir, you already gave us the background on how it is used in the construction of this base and the chemical makeup of moon soil."

Marcus looked at the boy. "I have? Well, have I mentioned solar radiation?" There were nods among the kids.

"What about oxygen generation?" He carefully watched his interns. "NASA and many of the Earthbound space agencies use a piece of machinery called the Environmental Control and Life Support System, or ECLSS. Water is processed into oxygen and hydrogen. This is the primary reason so much water is sent into space. Up here, water is life. Over on the International Space Station, they process human urine into the air they breathe first before processing any pure water."

"Eeew! Is that really true, Marcus?" Tina made a face at him.

"It's completely true, Tina. In space, nothing is wasted. All resources are a precious commodity. That is the main reason we are cleaning up the moon. By the look on all of your faces, you never considered where your bodily waste goes, did you? Let's talk about that, shall we?"

PAUL AND ANDERLE

✠ ✠ ✠

"Ugh! I'm never eating or drinking again! I can just taste it." Maxim had a disgusted look on his face.

Yana started to laugh. "We've been among these people for months, and you are just now wondering these things? Back home we did similar. Night soil was used as fertilizer for crops as well as tanning hides. Grow up, Maxim."

"How did they get all the water we use up here? Marcus never did explain that part." Ron now had more respect for those that grew the food he ate.

"Mom told me some of this. It's one of the reasons they hate us down there. The Queen ordered entire icebergs lifted up to us. She did pick ones that were navigational hazards to avoid damaging ships."

"If they were a danger why care about it?" Maxim could only stare at Tina.

"Natural resources were being stolen, or at least that is what the environmental groups all screamed. The bergs were in the ocean, but that didn't matter to them."

Ron looked over at Nestor. "What did the Queen do? Did she stop taking them?"

"The ones at sea she did. A couple of the countries in South America and those near the Arctic actually offered to sell them to her. Mom said she agreed and gave them what they wanted in exchange. There is a place that she took me once in the bowels of the Meredith Reynolds that is a giant pool of water. Some of the water they found out in the asteroid field is in there, too. Mom says some comets are nothing but frozen water and that there are plans to intercept and capture them."

Yana smiled at her young friend. "Maybe your mom

should come talk to us."

"I'll ask her," Tina agreed.

"Who are you asking?" Bobcat stuck his head into the room.

"Hi, Bobcat. Yana asked if we could get mom to talk to us sometime."

"Your mom is one of the hardest working women up there, but I bet if you asked nicely, she would do it. So, Marcus tells me you want to get out of here for a bit. Thanks for that. I won an ounce of gold off William on how long you could stand Marcus's lectures without running away. He does like to ramble."

All the kids nodded yes. Maxim rolled his eyes while doing so.

"So, we have three LRVs outside. I like to call them Moon Buggies. The engineers that were here one time souped them up pretty good. New batteries, transmissions, and structural enhancements make up the majority of improvements. How would you all like to take them for a spin?"

All the kids had big smiles on their faces. A day out of here!

"There are a few rules, of course. The LRVs have locator beacons on them as well as a travel radius of about fifty miles. Use the solar panels, or you will run out of juice earlier than intended. Use the radios and call us if you run into any trouble or find any tech we might have missed. Get your helmets and survival packs. I'll show you how to drive them."

Bobcat had to jump out of the way, or he would have been knocked to the floor. The five kids jumped up and hit the ground running. Scrambling out of the improvised lecture hall, they all but ran to their quarters to their stuff.

"We actually get to drive on the moon!" Ron found his

helmet and survival pack under his bed. The new and very cool TQB skinsuits didn't normally use a helmet. A special shield would snap into place if the suit were exposed to space or toxins such as gas. The helmet was an accessory that was added if you were space walking or used on planetary surfaces. Asteroid miners and other heavy duty positions used a hard suit that enclosed the entire body.

Maxim pulled his helmet off the top of a box and inspected it carefully. "Is good. Mother Russia never put a man on the moon, and now here I am! Is good." Carefully he attached the helmet and activated the seal.

"Too bad the Government won't care. They only want us dead and technology under their control. It is good we're not around anymore." Nestor put on his helmet, too.

Yana nodded her head in the boy's direction. "What do you think, Tina?"

"We need some time out of this box, so let's go." Tina glanced up at the curved roof and shuddered. She was just a tiny bit claustrophobic.

All five of them finished snapping the helmets into place and went to the main airlock near the flight deck. Using the safety protocols, they checked that each other's helmet was properly fastened.

Bobcat and William were waiting for them.

"Got your gravity shoes? Without them, you will be like superman and fly off into the sky. The only difference is he could come back down. If you forgot them, now is the time to tell me. How about helmets? Got one of those? Wonderful." William gave him a push and motioned counting money. Bobcat just shook his head.

"Everyone get their helmets on properly? There should be two small green lights up in the far corner of your HUD.

If you don't see them, tell me now."

None of the kids stirred.

"Good. Those lights signify that the seal on your helmet is good and that you are connected to the sensor package. Your suit can sense if the air is breathable as well as toxins or lack of atmosphere. You navigate using your eyes and tongue. It takes practice, so keep to the basics for now. In the lower right should be the communicator. It will detect radio frequencies and auto connects to other helmets. Non-TQB frequencies can be detected, but it takes a fine hand or a special comms helmet to understand them." Bobcat looked around to see if everyone was paying attention. He found five sets of eyes staring back at him.

"Great. Let's go outside." He waved at William who pressed a couple of buttons on the wall. A loud 'whooshing' noise could be heard as all the oxygen was sucked out of the landing bay. The bulkhead door to outside opened with a powerful *clang*.

The surface around the base was rocky and uneven. Piles of regolith and moon rock were everywhere. Construction of the base required explosives, and they had made a mess of the surface area. Directly outside the door all three LRV were lined up and ready to go.

Bobcat jumped up onto the first one in line. "Can everyone hear me OK?" All the kids including William responded.

"Now. Each of these can hold two people and a total cargo of around five hundred pounds. If by chance you find something bigger than that, mark it on your map, and we will use a pod to get it. You, boys, are stronger than humans, but let's not overdo it... OK? These suckers drive like regular cars now. The solar panel is an upgrade and can recharge the entire battery in a couple of hours if needed. My suggestion is to leave it deployed unless it's bouncing around too much. Top speed on these is around fifteen miles an hour. You can take two of them, so pick one."

Bobcat jumped off the rover and bounded over to William. They both watched as the kids kicked the tires and peered into the engine compartment. The engineers that upgraded the buggies painted names on them, Wheelie, Rota-Ree, and Dr. Crankinstein.

"Hey, Bobcat? What do the names mean?" Tina was crouched down behind Wheelie.

"Even I had to look that one up. Blame the engineers. It's an old cartoon program they thought fit these things."

"Oh, OK. Cool. We would like to take Wheelie and Rota-Ree, can we just go?"

"Not just yet. Use your tablets to navigate. Just northwest of us is the Mare Crisium area. That is marked on your maps as a No-Go area. There is a large amount of electromagnetic interference coming from there. It may cause a dropout in communications. Stay away from it. Everywhere else is open to you. Have fun, but stay alert and learn something. Now get out of here!"

Yana and Tina grabbed the pink colored LRV with the name Rota-Ree painted on a flag hanging off the back. Yana slapped Tina's hands off the wheel and checked over the controls. Someone had thoughtfully labeled everything and decorated every empty surface with pastel flowers. "I'm driving. You navigate."

Putting the little buggy in gear, Yana backed up and began to test out the simple controls.

Maxim, Nestor, and Ron had much more trouble.

"Why do I have to ride in the back?" Ron was tossed into the back by the much larger boys. He now was scrambling to find something to hold on to.

The controls on Wheelie were far more complicated. The engineers thought a jacked-up chassis and wheels fifty percent larger than standard was a good thing. Driving through the regolith and rock was similar to driving on soft sand or very deep snow.

"Ugh, this drives like Father's old truck!" Maxim shifted to another gear as the buggy's wheels sank into the soil.

"Your father's truck was more comfortable and bigger!" The two larger boys were crammed into the front seats. Neither of them had room to breathe.

"Good luck and have fun! Try to stay out of trouble." Bobcat's voice came over the speaker in their helmets as both buggies slipped and slid out of the base's entrance.

Watching them leave, Bobcat turned to William. "Half an ounce of gold they get into trouble within an hour, and we have to save them."

Before William could respond, another jumped into their conversation, "They are smarter than that, Bobcat. Give them at least two hours." Both men turned to see Marcus standing behind them.

Bobcat shook his head, "Ya think? I stick with an hour."

William looked between the two of them and shrugged. "Why not? You're on. Both of you. I'll take over two hours before trouble occurs."

All three men began to chuckle.

Just outside the base the boys in Wheelie were just starting to get the hang of the controls and were trying to catch up with the girls.

PAUL and ANDERLE

"Hey, Ron! Where are we going?" Nestor looked back at the young human who was sliding around the small cargo compartment.

"Hold on a minute." Ron grabbed the side of the rover and locked his gravity boots down using the helmet controls. They acted like giant magnets and secured him in place.

Ron, from his position in the back, couldn't tell their location. Pulling out his tablet, he punched the locator and waited. High overhead, one of the E.I.'s deployed in the over-watch satellite zeroed in on the signal and sent an update to his tablet in microseconds.

"We are in the Mare Vaporum crater headed toward the Sea of Tranquility." He was shouting when he didn't have to. Concentrating for a moment, he turned his mic down.

"Sorry guys."

"Is OK. Do you know where girls are headed?" Nestor looked back at him and smiled.

Ron said, "The girls are going to the Sea of Tranquility where Ranger 8 crashed, and Apollo 11 landed."

"Apollo 11? Like the movie?" Nestor's eyes widened. "Neil Armstrong, the first human on the moon?"

Ron laughed. "Yes, to all of those. Except they shot the movie back on Earth. We need to make sure they don't drive over the footsteps!"

"Why not call them?" Maxim asked.

Nestor and Ron looked at Maxim as he swerved to miss a large chunk of rock. "What did you say?"

Maxim snorted. "Call them. Didn't Bobcat say helmets auto-connect to other helmets?"

"That's not quite what he said, but … I'm an idiot. Thanks, Maxim!" Ron smiled, realizing that he could just call the girls.

"Potato, potahto is all the same. Hold on... big crater!

Yaaahooo!" The large boy let out an ear-piercing howl as the rover went off the edge of the large crater.

Half a mile to the west the girls were flying along. Rota-Ree had some speed to her.

"That's pretty." Tina pointed to a rock formation on their left.

"It looks like a dragon. We should get a picture, if anything, to show Team Charlie. They keep lording it up about space walking."

"That sounds good, Yana. We should do that. Remind me on the way back." Tina heard a faint scratching in her helmet.

"Did you hear that?"

Yana slowed the rover down and concentrated on the faint scratching only to be almost flattened by Maxim's howl!

CHAPTER TEN

What did you idiots do to this thing?" Yana was walking around Wheelie, shaking her head. The front end was smashed in along with the upper roll bars. It was a miracle the boys survived the crash.

"We drove off edge up there." Maxim pointed up to the edge of the large crater they were standing in.

Ron looked up, too. "Yeah, Maxim let out a howl and over we went! If my boots weren't locked to the deck, I might have died. Is it wrong to want to go again?"

Laughing, Maxim clapped Ron on his shoulder. "Nyet! We can find more, less dangerous things to do. Come. We fix."

"We fix. We fix. Is that all you have to say?" Nestor crawled out from under the rover. Grabbing his cousin's hand, he hauled himself to his feet.

"Is fixed?"

"Of course. Only a bent axle. We should be OK now. The body needs work, but is driveable."

"Good." Maxim saw the looks on the girls' faces. "Nestor is the family mechanic. Can fix anything mechanical. Where would you like to go?"

"Yana was taking me to see the Apollo 11 site, but I'm not so sure now." Tina pulled out her tablet.

"Tina, we are here." Ron stepped over and showed her his map. "Apollo 11 is way over there." He pointed.

"What is here?" Yana looked over Tina's shoulder.

"That is Palus Somni." Ron checked his own tablet. "It's right on the edge of the area they told us to stay out of."

"Why is it brown rather than gray?" Yana peered closer at the tablet.

"Not sure. My tablet doesn't have that information. The name means 'Marsh of Sleep.' It does have more of an albedo than the surrounding area. That might be the magnetic soil Bobcat mentioned."

"Ron, what is this 'albedo' you speak of?" Maxim had his tablet out too.

"In the simplest terms, it means a reflective surface. Many conspiracy groups think the shiny parts of the moon contain alien bases or ships. From Earth, all they can see is the reflection. If NASA has found anything, they didn't tell anyone."

"We should go look." The whole group turned to stare at Tina.

"I thought it was against the rules?" Yana grinned at her friend.

"They said it was off-limits because of weird electromagnetism. We could just go to the edge. Just to look."

Maxim gave Ron a push. "Well?"

"It's pretty far. These things go way faster than Bobcat

told us. Let me check the battery charges." He stepped over to the pink rover first.

Yana watched as Ron checked the battery and then deployed the solar panel. He came back and had to crawl under his beat-up rover.

"I deployed your panels. We have enough juice to get us there, but we might not have enough to get back. It does get dark here. We might have to call them to save us."

"Still big adventure and way worth it. What do you say, Yana?" Maxim stared at his competition.

"Only if your buggy runs. If not, we will abort and give them a call. Understood?"

"Understood. It'll run. Nestor is a master fixer." Maxim and his cousin climbed into the rover.

"Hey, what about me?" Ron stared up at his friends.

"You ride with girls this time, Ron. The rover is too dangerous now." Maxim turned the key, and they could all hear the whine of the electric motor.

"It will start." Nester motioned with his chin for Maxim to give it some 'gas.'

The rover lurched forward very shakily. Up in the cockpit, the boys were bouncing around more than usual, but mostly safe.

"Boys!" Yana said, "Ron, hop on in." They all climbed into Rota-Ree and took off after the monster truck version of a moon rover.

With a goal now in mind, the two rovers started to make better time than before. The Wheelie vehicle was a tiny bit slower than the girl's rover due to the crash. Nestor's quick fix wasn't perfect.

Nestor nudged his cousin, "Maxim, you were too harsh with Ron."

"He scared me when we landed in the crater. I thought for sure he was dead. I was looking for his body when he tapped me on the arm. I must have jumped a foot. He is a good friend, I will apologize later."

"You do that. This is fun." Nestor was watching the craters and rocks on the surface. For all his nonchalance, this was really cool. They were on the Moon!

"I'm tempted just to leave all this stuff and have Jean destroy it from orbit." Bobcat was under one of the computer consoles trying to unhook the system.

He heard William from above, "Why do that? You said it yourself, this equipment is important."

"I know that, but they made this stuff so close to the wall I can't quite reach it!" His arm was up into the middle of the wires and cables.

"Move your arm."

There was a muffled grunt. "What did you say?"

"Bobcat, move your arm!"

He pulled his arm back and asked. "Why?" A large machete came swinging along the wall just missing his head.

"Aaaiiee!" Bobcat yelled, and scooted out of the tiny space. "You just missed hitting me!"

"I was careful." William checked the blade before putting it away.

"Where did you get that thing, and why is it up here on the moon?" Bobcat checked his hair and top of his head with his fingers.

"I don't go anywhere without it. Ever since those guys shot me, I try to stay armed." He patted the large blade again.

"With that? From what? Rogue asteroids? You are crazy, man."

"We can re-wire this stuff later, and besides, it saves a bunch of time." William started packing up the now disconnected, equipment.

"This might be easier with those kids helping. Have you been watching them?" Bobcat placed the chopped-up wire into one of the recycling bags.

"Me? I thought you were doing that," William closed the box.

Bobcat scratched his chin, "No. I thought we agreed, you would keep an eye on them. Maybe it was Marcus."

"Maybe it was Marcus, what?" Marcus stepped over some of the equipment and began peeking into the equipment bays.

"Keeping an eye on the kids. You've been tracking them, right?" Bobcat stopped what he was doing and stared at the older scientist.

"No. Was I supposed to? I left that up to you two since you turned them loose."

"Guys, if I didn't watch them and you didn't watch them… Where are they now?" William had his tablet out and was staring at it.

"OK, I'll play. Where are they?" Bobcat looked over at his best friend.

William mumbled, "That was rhetorical. I think that teacher lady is right. We should call you Bozo. They aren't showing up on my map." He held up the tablet and turned it around for Bobcat to see.

"What? Please don't tell me we lost them." Bobcat reached for the tablet and stared at it.

Looking at his own Marcus began to make faces at it. "I know where they were."

"Where?" Bobcat asked.

"They went toward the Sea of Tranquility. It looks like the girls got ahead of the boys somehow, and they went through this section here to catch up." Marcus pointed at the map.

"Ouch! That is a huge drop-off! Are they dead? Please tell me they aren't dead. The Queen is going to kill me! Cheryl Lynn will kill me, and John is definitely going to kill me, probably twice. Have you seen him lately? I think he has grown to extra-large-and-deadly. It will be chiseled on my gravestone I am the only member of Team BMW to be killed," he started counting on his fingers, "Four times!" Bobcat held his head and began to moan.

"Not dead. See, they started moving again. They were headed toward the Marsh of Sleep, that's right on the edge of where we told them not to go." Marcus tried to zoom in closer. Bobcat let go of his head and stepped over to look.

William shrugged, "Of course. Tell them not to go, and they do anyway. They should still be on the map. We've flown over that area before without harm. It is a bit shaky, but doable." Bobcat's breathing had slowed down, but he was still trying not to hyperventilate.

"That's in a pod. Who knows what it's like on the ground. We need to look for them." William stared at his friends.

"We can use the E. I. satellite system to look for them. If we ask ADAM or Meredith to help, we should find them pretty quick." Marcus pulled his tablet back from Bobcat and began to type.

"Marcus, what are you doing?" Bobcat gave him a funny look.

"Sending a message up to the Meredith Reynolds asking for ADAM or TOM to take a look." He began to type faster. Suddenly his tablet was snatched out of his hands.

Marcus looked up confused, "Why did you do that? I was almost finished."

"Dude, we can't ask for help! We have to do it, just us. If they find out about it, up there...We will never live it down. We will be the ones that lost five kids on their first field trip! We have to find them ourselves."

"Marcus, Bobcat is right. I can't believe it either, but the Queen won't be very happy with us if we lose them. We can use the pod to carry the last rover. We can trace where they went and then follow their tracks. They are kids."

William looked at his two friends, "How hard can it be?"

"Whoa! Look out for that boulder!" The Marsh of Sleep was a bust. The soil was just a brown rust color that looked to be the result of a meteor impact. Ron was taking samples when they saw the gleam.

Twenty minutes earlier...

"So, it's just one big impact crater?" Tina stood in the middle of what resembled a brown field of rocks.

"The different colored stones are what makes the color show up from space. The meteor must have been massive to cause this much debris." Ron picked up rocks here and there, adding them to his bag.

"So, where to now?" Yana casually looked all around her.

Nestor pointed toward the east. "What is that? It appears to be moving."

"A spacecraft or probe of some kind? It could be Marcus and Bobcat looking for us." Maxim dug in the rover for something to see better with.

"Let's go check it out. It's just over there." Ron pointed. "It might be wreckage or something we can haul back."

"He's got a point." Tina agreed. "If we find wreckage, they won't yell so much about us going out-of-bounds."

"Tina, you rule breaker you. Come on boys, let's go find the whatever-it-is." Yana waved them to the rovers.

"Sure. Why not. We are overdue anyway." Maxim climbed behind the wheel again.

The gleam in the distance suddenly disappeared.

"Hey, it's gone! Maybe it was a probe." Ron strained his eyes to see.

"Let's go anyway." The two rovers continued east.

"I'm starting to hate these kids." William stared at the hole dug out of the regolith where a rover obviously crashed.

Bobcat punched his friend in the arm. "Don't hate the kids."

Rubbing his shoulder William replied. "I don't really hate them. They just make me look bad. That fall should have destroyed that rover. But somehow, they fixed it and continued on. They could take my job, that's all."

"They went east, like on the map." Marcus pointed toward the tracks. "The larger rover is driving a little shaky."

"OK, now I don't feel so bad. They aren't perfect. Are you sure they are headed to the Marsh of Sleep?"

Marcus nodded. "That is where the computer lost them. The EM field is much stronger than it was last year. I will have to check the older readings." He began to type on his tablet.

"Um, Marcus, what are you doing?"

PAUL AND ANDERLE

Marcus looked up noticing his two friends stared at him. "Uh, I was checking last year's findings and comparing them. I was about to have ADAM… Oh. Sorry. I forgot."

Bobcat waved his hands in the air and shook his head. "Just kill me already, Marcus. Thanks, buddy."

Their Pod swooped over the brown colored area known as the Marsh of Sleep by those on Earth. Not a kid in sight.

"OK, now what?" Bobcat looked to William.

"We drop the LRV and search for them. We can lock the pod's position down, it will stay here for us." He carefully set the Pod down on the brown soil.

"Have either of you driven one of these rovers?" Marcus climbed into the rear of the vehicle.

"I have, but only to move it. This one is Dr. Crankinstein, according to the artwork on the back." The rover was painted like it belonged to the Munsters.

"Are the other two decorated like this?" Marcus examined the skulls and spiders decorating the rear area.

"Not quite. Those engineers we sent here were a bit on the odd side. I think this one was painted by a goth or something." The steering wheel was off of a race car. Both it and the gear stick were skull shaped.

"I like it. Remind me to track this guy down. He can decorate my car for me." William smiled.

"What car? The one back in Florida that the State confiscated? That car?"

"They confiscated his car? Where was I when this happened?" Marcus looked at William.

"It was around the same time they got BA's house in Smugglers Cove. They called it eminent domain, but you know they were looking for tech or clues about TQB. I'm going to miss my car the most. It was sweet!"

ALPHA CLASS

William's face took on a darker look. "A buddy of mine in the police force told me they stripped it down and used saws to cut it apart. Haven't they ever seen a lift kit before? Idiots."

"I'm not up on my cars, but what did you have?" Marcus knew guys liked to talk about cars.

"It was a 1968 Road Runner my dad left me. All original. I jacked it up in the back. Added chromed bumpers, wheels, and custom tailpipes. That car was my baby." He looked away for a moment.

"Sorry for your loss." Marcus put his arm on William's just as the rover began to shake.

"What is going on?"

"Don't look at me! I was going to ask you!" William pulled his hands off the wheel as the rover began to be pulled in a new direction.

CHAPTER ELEVEN

I could almost swear this was where we saw that flash of metal." Ron stood next to the pink rover looking out at the endless, shadow-filled landscape.

"Ron, does the rover have enough power to get us back to base? We're really far away." Tina fiddled with the power monitoring controls, which unlike everything else, weren't labeled. Yana looked concerned at her friend.

"What does the monitor say? It's the readout bar on the left-hand side."

"We have full bars on that one. The one in the middle is all red." Tina thumped it with her fingers trying to make the readout move.

"That is the recharge rate. Red is bad. We need to check the other rover." He scanned the horizon trying to spot the moon version of a monster truck.

Yana called out to the rest of the team. "Maxim? Can you hear me?"

"Nestor? Come in please?" All three kids could hear a faint scratching in their helmets.

"Are these things defective?" Tina rolled her eyes as she tried to get the helmet to run a diagnostic.

"Bobcat said they were new, but they tested them extensively out in the asteroid belt, so they should work. It might be that EM field we were warned about. We may have to drive closer to them." Ron rolled his eyes along with his friend.

"Get back in the car, Ron. We will chase the boys." Giving the tech-savvy boy time to climb on, she started the electric engine and gave the accelerator a nudge.

The pink rover took off in the direction the monster truck was last seen.

Pop! Crackle… sssssss. "All I get is static. I thought there was something there for a moment." Nestor stuck out his tongue and wiggled it.

Maxim chuckled at his cousin. "That makes you look funny. Too bad I haven't a camera. I think you must roll your eyes to fine tune the sound."

"Not what I was doing. I saw a tab for location and mapping. Bobcat said there were more advanced features. I was trying to access them." He stuck out his tongue and appeared to lick his nose.

"So? Did you find them?"

"Maybe. I have a map on my HUD now. The blinking icon shows three somethings headed in our direction. Should we wait?"

"Da. I mean yes. We wait. English is… hard. We wait for others." Maxim turned the rover off and checked the batteries.

His readout showed only a trickle of energy recharging now. Thankfully, the batteries were full.

"You think Ron found something yet?" Nestor slumped in his seat and scratched an imaginary itch he couldn't reach.

"Possibly. He is smart. Did you know about some of what he speaks about?"

"Some. Mainly the mechanical aspects. Do you remember the trip I took with Father to Moscow when I was ten?"

Maxim thought for a moment then nodded. "Yes. Your father asked us to take care of the farm for you."

"When his business was over we went to the Museum of Cosmonautics. He wanted me to learn about how humans can overcome things. He wanted me to never underestimate people. He said it would save my life one day. But the museum was like a dream. The machines and rockets made me want to learn to take them apart and build more. It was fantastic!" Nestor's eyes shined with remembrance.

"Was that the summer you blew up the goat barn?"

"That was an accident. Too much alcohol in the rocket fuel mix. Father was not pleased. He destroyed all my experiments and told me to never attempt it again."

"He wanted to protect you. Too much attention might be drawn our way. Boris could only protect us so much. You know that." Maxim looked over at his cousin.

"I know that now. But as a child I was heartbroken. Space was out of reach for me. This... this fills me with wonder. What does the future hold for us if this is just the first few weeks of school?" Nestor waved his arms in a circle.

"Not blowing up a barn? We will learn everything we can, so one day we can help a small ten-year-old boy who wants to go to space."

Catching a flash of light out of the corner of his eye

Maxim pointed. "There they are. Yana, can you hear me?"

"Yana... hear..."

"Did you catch that, Ron?" Yana jerked the wheel to the left to miss a small crater.

"Yes. I have them pinpointed. According to my helmet, they are north of us about ten degrees. I think the problem is the EM field. It's weird, it increases in strength the closer to the crater center we get."

"Guys, I see what I think is them up ahead." Tina pointed toward the same direction Yana was already driving.

Peering through the growing gloom, Ron could just make out the shape of the beat-up rover. "Maxim, do you hear us?"

"It's about time you caught up to us. Nice to hear another voice!" Maxim replied.

"We looked, and you guys were gone. Did you find any sign of wreckage or anything?"

"Nothing, Ron. We searched the area and found exactly nothing. The sun going down worried us. Do we have enough power to get back?"

"I don't think we do. We could combine the batteries and make it, but will either of the rovers hold five people? Nestor, what do you think?"

The two rovers were now in sight of each other. Everyone smiled and waved.

"We weigh too much. One option is Maxim and I could follow on foot and let you three use the rover."

"Nyet! No. We stay together. Nestor that is a bad idea. Find another option." Yana put her foot down firmly.

Tina, Ron, Nestor, and Yana started trying to figure out

options for them as Maxim surveyed the area. All he could see was the outline of distant craters and rocks. According to the helmet maps, they were right on the edge of Mare Crisium or the Sea of Crisis. The crater seemed to be the source of the EM field that was affecting all communications. Strangely enough, they could talk now when they couldn't before. Maxim looked toward the east and his eyes widened.

"Yana."

Yana and the others were in deep discussions over where to put the batteries from Rota-Ree on Wheelie and still have room for extra passengers. They didn't hear Maxim's quiet voice.

"Yana! Stop talking!" Maxim finally had to yell.

Yana turned toward the large boy and glared. "Maxim Nikolayevich what gives you the right to interrupt me at this time? We need to figure out how to get back!"

"None of that matters now. Look!" He pointed toward the East.

The center of the crater was glowing.

"What is that? Is it Bobcat and the others?" Yana stared at the greenish-blue glow.

"I don't think so. They should be coming from the west. That is something else." Tina pointed behind them.

Ron glanced at the glow like the others, but only as a distraction. He still measured the battery compartment on Wheelie to see if Rota's would fit when the tool he was using flew out of his hand.

Ron could only stare at his empty hand as yet another of the box of tools flew off. "Hey, guys?"

The tools spread out on the rear of the rover were now flying off into the night toward the green glow. The toolbox began to rattle and jump. "Guys!"

All heads turned in Ron's direction just in time to see the toolbox lift out of the rover and become airborne.

"Ron! What's happening?"

"No time to explain, Tina! Maxim, we need to all get in the rovers, or we may never see them again!" The rovers, like the toolbox, began to rattle and shake. Wheelie began to noticeably slide sideways.

"The magnetic field is pulling us in! We need to either get in or lose the rovers!" Everyone piled into their rovers and tried to steer toward the anomaly.

"Hold on, here we go." Maxim unlocked the brakes and steered toward the center of the crater.

Both rovers were pulled toward the middle of the crater by a force that didn't seem to belong to nature. The speedometer on Yana's rover registered a speed of over fifty miles per hour. More than twice that of its previous speed. Ahead of them, they could see the glow had increased.

"Any idea of what is ahead?" Tina looked over her shoulder at Ron.

He shook his head, "No. It has to be using some sort of tractor beam. It must have activated because of our communications. Notice, it was only after we got together did it activate."

The crater's center came into view. A small, dome-shaped, lump was at the exact center. Dark tunnel shaped spaces were open around the edges. The tunnels seemed to be their destination. The incline became much steeper as they were pulled down.

All five kids screamed in terror as they were pulled into the dark. The rovers continued down and over, what appeared to be a steep cliff.

"Aaiiee" echoed in their helmet as the rovers went over

the edge and stopped suddenly with a resounding crunch of metal and plastic.

Maxim and Nestor were thrown from Wheelie as it tumbled down into a pile of metal. The girls, belted and buckled into the rover, had passed out and were hanging upside down in a pile of what appeared to be spacecraft parts.

"Hello? Did everyone survive? Maxim?" Ron called out to his friends. His magnetic boots saved him for the second time, but he was now hanging upside down staring at the ground.

"I cannot move." Maxim groaned in pain.

"I'll help as soon as I get free, hold on!" Ron called back.

"Find the girls, Ron. I will heal; it is just painful. Nestor? You alive?"

"Ugh. Did you get the name of the truck that hit us? Go punch him for me." Nestor found himself in a pile of what looked like probes and scrap metal. "Where are we?"

Maxim felt the bones in his arms and legs knitting and painfully sat up. He looked up at the glowing ceiling of the area. "We are in the crater, but it is not a crater. Looks like a spacecraft."

Their rover was lying on top of a pile of white, gold, and gray painted scrap metal. Behind, was the pink Rota-Ree rover. Maxim could see Ron trying to climb up to release the girls.

"Ron, I can see you. Be careful. They will fall if they're asleep when you release them. Nestor, can you help Ron?"

"Possibly. I am wedged underneath what looks to be an LK lander."

"Nestor, that's impossible! The Soviets never put one on the moon."

"I am under one, so it is possible, Ron. I can see the

Soviet markings complete with hammer and sickle on the side. Let me get free first, and then we can explore. Hold on a moment."

Both boys could hear the sound of metal crashing as Nestor broke free of his temporary prison. "I am free."

"Nestor, I just need someone to catch the girls if they fall. There is gravity down here somehow. I just about have Tina's seatbelt free."

"Ron, look down." Ron looked down and saw Nestor with his arms open. "Great. I have to cut through the belt, get ready to catch her."

The emergency seat belts on the rover were never designed to hold a person inside if it turned over, but they held anyway. Ron needed to use his survival knife to cut them loose. The locking mechanism was completely frozen.

Tina could hear voices talking about her and saying her name as she started to wake up. The last thing she remembered was screaming into the night as the rover went down into the dark. The sensation of falling was not something she enjoyed. She shook her head to clear the cobwebs and thought she heard "…catch her."

"Ron? Wait, I'm awwAAAAake!" Tina screamed a second time as she dropped free of the rover.

"Oof!" Nestor caught the smaller girl in his arms and held onto her now squirming body. "It's me, Tina. It's me!"

"What the hell, Nestor? What did you do that for?" She popped him in the shoulder with her fist as he set her down.

"I just did what Ron said to do." He pointed up at Ron.

She looked up, "The hell, Ron! You could have woken me up first!"

"We didn't want you to get hurt falling from up here. Sorry?" Ron had one leg braced on what was an LK lander. His hands held Yana's shoulder as he tried to free her from the rover above him.

"Wow! That's pretty high up. You are forgiven." She punched Nestor again.

"What was that for?"

Tina gave him a stern look. "Think of it as a lesson learned. Ron, try to wake Yana up first."

"What lesson?" Nestor asked. Tina chose not to answer and ignored him.

Ron gave Yana a rather awkward shake from the upside-down position he was in. "Yana, can you hear me?"

"What do you want, Ron?" Yana opened her eyes and let out a small scream. "Why am I upside down?"

Shifting his foot to another, less shaky position, Ron stepped a tiny bit closer to her. "Yana, this is your choice. Do you want me to drop you down to Nestor and let him catch you? Or do you want to try and climb down yourself?"

Ron pulled out his knife again and made cutting motions where she could see him.

"Drop me." She closed her eyes and screamed as she plunged down out of the buggy.

CHAPTER TWELVE

What is all this stuff?" Tina poked at a partially crushed machine that looked like a series of globes connected with legs and structural bars.

"The writing looks Cyrillic." Ron walked over to stand next to her.

"Russian? Let me look." Yana peered closer at the writing. "It's mostly destroyed, but it says Luna something."

"Could it be fifteen that you can't read?" Ron bent down and brushed at the letters.

"That would fit, wouldn't it?" Nestor joined the small group.

Ron pointed at the LK Lander Nestor crashed into. "It would. It makes me wonder about the rest of all this including that over there."

"I've seen one of those before in Moscow. There is nothing at the museum about actually landing on the moon."

"What are you two talking about?" Tina stepped in front of the two boys.

"Luna 15 was launched by the Soviets at the same time America was landing Apollo 11 here, on the moon. It crashed during its landing in Mare Crisium. This thing, however, shouldn't exist here. According to history, the Soviets ended their lunar program in 1970 and never actually landed on the moon." Ron reached over and laid his hand on the lander.

"Making sure it's real?" Yana smiled at the younger boy.

"Sort of. This is one of the later models. They designed them for one pilot. Its presence here makes me wonder if he's in there or somewhere else?"

"Can we check?" The LK Lander was at least fifteen feet tall, its spidery legs looked to be still intact, but a bit bent. Small satellite dishes and other devices hung off arms attached to the main body of the lander.

"The touchdown pressure engines have fired." Nestor pointed to large pods with char marks, attached to the legs of the bulbous lander.

"So, it appears to have landed safely. The folding ladder's been deployed, so someone has either gone in or out of it. It only held one cosmonaut... So, who wants to go first?" Nestor looked at the three members of his group.

"I would like to." Everyone turned to see Maxim picking his way out of the debris. Nestor high-fived his cousin.

"Are you better now?" Yana looked him over, carefully checking his suit for tears.

"I'm fine. I think I should go, since I did bounce off it, breaking my bones. Wechselbalg. Crack us, beat us up, but we just heal back together again. Do you think it's occupied?"

Nestor popped open some of the survival boxes attached to the lander and looked inside. "These are empty. He may have survived the landing. Go ahead and look."

Maxim grabbed the ladder and pulled himself up. The gravity was at about half, so it was easy to do. The circular hatch was slightly ajar.

Knocking on the side of the hatch to announce his presence, Maxim opened the door. "It's empty. Someone was here, though."

"What's up there?" Ron almost climbed the ladder himself.

"Lots of empty ration packs, air bottles, and some sort of mission log. Give me a moment." The inside of the capsule was tiny and very clunky in design. The cosmonaut would have had to stand or lean for most of the mission. There was almost no room even to think of getting out of the spacesuit. Maxim just shook his head. Brave men.

"Here." He handed the book to Yana as he climbed down. Ron jumped on the ladder and went up for a look.

Yana carefully opened the mission log. It was two pieces of aluminum holding several dozen pages of handwritten notes. She rapidly read through it.

"This is insane." She looked at the others after a moment.

"Why? I guess he survived the landing?" Tina took the book from her hand. She learned some Russian in school, but her understanding of the written language was poor.

"He survived. The mission was a secret, he and his partner were volunteers. Russia wanted to say they landed on the moon, too, and he was to be the first. The mission was successful until he landed. They picked this location because of the details the Luna 15 sent. His communications failed as soon as the lander touched down. Despite swapping out his batteries and realigning the dishes, he couldn't connect to his partner in orbit. The ascent propulsion unit failed to deploy, and he was unable to access the electronics to check it. He logged several moonwalks here as he tried to fix the craft."

"Does he say what his name is, Yana?" Ron jumped off the ladder and walked over to them.

"It does. Andrei Mikoyan was his name. He mentions his partner 'Ivan,' but gives no last name or other identifying information. This mission was in 1972. Nestor, didn't you say the Soviet moon missions were over by then?"

"I did. At least that is what the museum said in Moscow. But we both know how accurate the Soviets are about history. This man can't possibly still be alive."

Tina laid her hand on Yana's arm. "What happened to him after the rockets failed?"

"He was getting desperate. He was about to attempt to take off his helmet and commit suicide when he felt the lander move on its own. Instead of going up, the vehicle was being dragged sideways. He looked out the door, but it was night, and the exterior lights wouldn't work. All he had was a very small amount of ambient light reflecting off of objects. The lander bounced and shuddered as it continued to move laterally until he found himself surrounded by wreckage. This document claims that he saw aliens moving around, and they went into a door in the central column. The last entry says his food, water, and oxygen were almost gone. He went in search of the aliens."

"Andrei may have been seeing things if his oxygen was failing. But, we have all heard of TOM, so maybe it was aliens." Ron looked at Yana. "Did he say anything else?"

"'Mother save me.' His last words were for his mother." A small tear made its way down Yana's face. "I don't want to die here like this man! We need to find a way out."

"Yana, honey, calm down. We don't know for sure we are

trapped yet. This is only a small part of the junkyard. That up there isn't natural, so maybe they are good aliens. Don't cry." Tina patted her on the back.

"Nestor, check out the batteries on the LK, see if we can use them. Ron, check the column and see if you see any trace of an opening or door. Tina, why don't you get Yana to sit a moment. I'm going to see if either rover is salvageable." Maxim said as he started to climb up the LK.

"I am fine Maxim. Stop babying me!" Yana refused to sit still.

"Fine. Why don't you and Tina look around and try to find something we can use to get out of here then?"

Back on board the QBBS Meredith Reynolds.

Diane closed the tablet and screens in front of her and looked at her sister. "Are all the kids back for the night?"

"Everyone except for Craig in Team Bravo and all of Alpha." Dorene checked her braid in the mirror as she spoke. The Academy had standards for everyone, even the directors wore uniforms and kept their hair according to the old military regulations.

"What happened to Craig? I didn't understand Jean's message on that one."

Dorene chuckled. "I shouldn't laugh. Kids getting hurt is never funny. Dr. Running Wolf gave him a lecture to go with the ear-burner Jean gave him. She had the kids out on the range testing the new personal side arms and human Guardian weapons. She had Rangemasters in place, and everyone was under supervision of course. Craig is from one of the

Midwestern Packs, Iowa I think. He thought he was tough and tried to fire the prototype for John's new guns after being told to leave it be."

Diane closed her eyes and winced. "Did Jean hurt him?"

"It wasn't Jean. Before anyone could notify her, he snuck it out onto the firing line and set it on level eight. He's very lucky he didn't put it on ten. As it is, they're already calling him stumpy."

"What happened?"

"Stupid kid blew his fingers right off. Those pistols have so much recoil, only the most advanced Guardians can even hold them. Jean told me even she hadn't fired them on full maximum."

"Where is Craig now?" Diane pulled out his file from her desk.

"He's in the main infirmary. Dr. Keelson says he'll live. Dr. Running Wolf told me about it, in detail. I sent you the medical and incident files for when you need the information. I also gave a copy of the Safety Report to Jean with the information on how he snuck the weapon out of the Armory. The Queen could speed up his healing, but everyone says she said he needed to learn a lesson about *No meaning No*."

"I can see that. So, where is Team Alpha?"

"Them? Marcus and Bozo took them down to the old moon base to dismantle it. I called a while ago, but only the E.I. answered. She said they were on a field trip to the EM field and communications were temporarily down. Whatever that means."

"I think I know the area. It was in the notes about the moon base. Remind me to touch base with them tomorrow. We need some sort of update on what they are learning. Just to make sure it's not paperwork again." Diane closed the tablet again and put them away.

"I can take a pod down and go terrorize Bozo again if you like?"

The redheaded twins both laughed for a moment. "You are too much woman for him. Leave him be for now. You can scare him later. So, how are the other classes doing so far?"

"Well Foxtrot is enjoying working with Jeo so far. He has them…"

"Did you find anything?" Ron and Tina compared notes.

"A lot of space junk. I think this is where old NASA equipment goes to die. Moon probes, a couple of rovers, a few Chinese probes, and what I swear is the remains of an LRV."

"You found another LRV?" Tina stared at him.

"It's over here. It just can't be here. They only brought up three of them." Ron led her through a pile of meteor bits and scrap metal that had the word 'NASA' on it. A classic moon rover lay upside down in the dirt of the crater. The smashed communications array lay in front of it. On the bottom, Tina could plainly see the hinge that allowed it to be folded to store inside the lander.

"It's real, Ron. NASA might have sent all sorts of things up here without telling anyone. Look at the Russian lander we found. What happened to Apollo 18, 19 and 20? Maybe this is from one of them."

Ron shook his head. "No. They canceled those. The landers are on display in museums. NASA's own documents say the LRV for 18 was used for spare parts. There is no record they built anymore."

"Ron, there is a hole in your logic. If they used the LRV

for spare parts, where did they use them? Now ask yourself, why would they need spare parts in the first place? Hmmm?" Tina gave him a questioning look.

"I… I don't know. I'll ask Yana about it. We need to get back." He pulled her toward where their own LRVs were located.

"I meant to ask you. Did you find any sign of aliens or a door on that thing?" Tina pointed at the huge column that held up whatever that was that was glowing.

"No. Not a single thing. I looked for drag marks, too. Yana said that Andrei might have been suffering from hypoxia. That would cause you to see things. Can you imagine going out into space with limited oxygen and supplies? Those men were some kind of brave."

"We are very lucky, Ron. These suits and the helmets would seem like magic to the early space explorers. The only thing I don't like are the rations. It's like eating toothpaste."

Ron laughed. "Nutritional substitutes. That is what Chef Norman called them. I had asked him before we left. According to him, they perfected the paste during the asteroid mining phase. Each of those tubes will keep you alive for a week."

"But do they have to taste so nasty?" Tina made a face at him.

"Mine are pretty good. What flavors have you been getting?"

"Hot and spicy ones. Thai noodle, Pad Thai with peppers, Pho, and a couple others I can't pronounce."

Ron laughed again. "When we packed, didn't you check the labels first?"

"There are labels? Where?"

"Food processing makes four different kinds of tubes for the survival packs and for mission food. Regular has things like meatloaf, spaghetti, and tuna casserole. Vegetarian has veggie dishes with tofu and beans for protein. International has a variety of countries and regions. They are labeled. I like the German ones the best. To me, it sounds like you got one of the Asian packs."

Tina made a face at him and stuck out her tongue. "What is the fourth type?"

"Chef Norman said that one was called a 'Special.' They are very bland flavors and foods that can be eaten by anyone, anywhere. He said they are used in rescue missions or trips down to Earth where they have to give food away. It's why all the governments down there think we are desperate for food up here."

She nodded her head. "I see. More of the Queen's tricks."

"Probably. Look there's Yana." He pointed up ahead.

"Hey, Yana, did you find anything?"

She turned to the two of them, "Define anything. I found lots of junk. Some of it doesn't look like it's from around here. Have either of you ever seen TOM's ship?"

"No. Mom has; she told me about it. Did you find a Kurtherian ship?"

Yana shook her head. "I have no idea. I found what looks like part of a saucer as well as a rocket with German writing on it. Did the Nazi's go into space? Because it has a swastika."

Ron just stared at her. "Not in any real history book I have ever read, but they did succeed in the conspiracy stories on the internet. We found another LRV out there that isn't supposed to exist either. Have you seen Maxim or Nestor? They should be around here still."

"Maxim and his cousin are over by our LRVs. They got them down, and Nestor is trying to combine the batteries." She joined them as they headed back.

PAUL AND ANDERLE

✤ ✤ ✤

"Will it work?" Maxim stared at his cousin's legs and feet. They were sticking out from under a much-battered Rota-Ree.

"I don't know. You've asked me the same question for an hour now. I've got them wired up, and according to the readouts, this goofy green light is recharging the batteries some. These, plus the ones off the Soviet relic over there, might be enough. If the others find a couple more, we would have enough to get back to the base. But. We still have to get up to the surface first."

Maxim replied, "One problem at a time, Cousin. Just fix the rover."

"I'm trying to. God, it's like talking to Fergus, the innkeeper's son. Remember him? He was like a post with feet."

"What happened to him?" Maxim resisted the temptation to hurry his cousin some more, again.

"He and his father didn't trust Boris, so they left town when the trouble started. There, I think I have it now." He pushed his way out from under the rover.

"I told you I could do it." Nestor batted Maxim's hands away as he engaged the engine. The pink rover thrummed to life.

There was a flash of light like a strobe, and the power died on the rover. "Hey what the hell?"

Both boys heard a whirring noise. They looked up and all around their area trying to track on the sound. Suddenly, out of the shadows, a large, black as night, metallic arm grabbed Maxim's leg.

✤ ✤ ✤

"It sounds like they are arguing again." Tina nudged Ron.

"They fight constantly. I'm surprised they haven't killed each other yet." Ron elbowed her back.

"They are cousins. It's how they show they care about each other. Just ignore it. I do." Yana smiled at them.

"By all the Gods of Earth and Sky! What is that?" Tina pointed at a large black shape appearing near the boys. As they watched, it attacked the boys.

Maxim felt something grab him, and he tried to jerk his leg away. The metallic arm held fast to his leg and started to drag him toward the central column. A door that had not been there before was now open. A bright, piercing light, shone out of the opening.

"Nestor! Help me." Maxim began to pummel the robot-like thing with his fists. Being a Were made him stronger than usual, and he was leaving dents on the metal surface.

Nestor ran to his cousin's aid and began to beat on the thing with a metal rod.

"Quick! Block that door open! It may be our only chance to get out of here!" Yana pointed at the door, yelling at Tina and Ron.

She grabbed a large rock and joined the others in beating on the robot appendage.

"Let." *Clang.* "My." *Clang.* "Friend." *Clang.* "Go!" *Clang.*

The robot released Maxim and waved its arms trying to escape from its tormentors. Aiming at the blinking lights, Nestor whacked it as hard as he could with the rod.

"Is it dead?" Yana hit it again just for good measure.

Nestor poked it with the rod. The whirring noise had stopped as well as all movement. "Looks like it is."

"Hey! Can we get some help here?" Tina's voice called out over the radios.

PAUL AND ANDERLE

Ron and Tina had rolled some large rocks in front of the doors, but the doors were still trying to close automatically.

Helping Maxim to stand, the others ran over and entered the small room that was lit with a white light.

"Are you sure we should go in here?" Ron stood outside, looking in.

"Come on, Ron, it's our only chance to get out of here." Tina reached out and grabbed his arm and yanked him in.

The doors, crushing the rocks blocking the exit, closed behind them.

CHAPTER THIRTEEN

You realize there could be more of those robots or killer aliens when this thing stops, right?" Ron nervously looked around at his friends.

"We can take em." Nestor still brandished the metal bar he picked up.

"Did anyone but me notice this elevator is going down and not up?" Yana, her hands moving over the walls, looked for a control panel.

Maxim kicked the door. "This must be some sort of base. It can't be Kurtherians then; they don't build bases." He looked over, "Do they, Tina?"

"What am I, the alien expert? I told you, I've heard TOM like once when I was with Marcus and he wasn't talking to me at the time. From what mom told me about the group in China they didn't build a base. They just let the human slaves do it for them."

PAUL AND ANDERLE

Without warning, the elevator stopped, and the doors re-opened.

Maxim stepped out first. The landing room was dark until his foot touched the floor. Lights came up revealing a rounded hallway leading off in two directions. Small lights sparkled here and there along the walls. "Come on, I think it's safe."

The other four members of the team joined Maxim as the doors to the elevator closed. There was a small blinking light on the wall next to where the door should be. Nestor poked at the light with his finger, and the door reopened.

"Hey, at least we can get back in the elevator!"

"Yeah, but we can't make it go up. We should keep searching." Maxim gave his cousin a nudge. "Good work finding the controls, though."

Ron fingered the textured walls and stared at the way it was constructed. "Why does this look like one of the tubes on *Star Journey*? Have you ever seen that show?"

"No TV in Russia, remember? What is this *Star Journey*?" Nestor stepped over next to him.

"It was about… It's hard to explain without showing you. We should go to one of the conventions sometime. You would make a good Chekov."

Nestor gave Ron a funny look. "This show is about playwrights? Why? I thought you said it was in space?"

"No, no not the playwright. This guy flew the ship and talked about wessels all the time."

"What is a wessel? It sounds like some sort of food. What were we talking about?'

Ron laughed. "I'm not sure anymore. Why do you think these are round?" He pointed at the tunnels.

"It could be the construction technique. I suppose we

could ask that over there." Nestor pointed to a robot that exited a door on the right and was gliding toward them at a fast pace.

"Maxim! Robot!"

Maxim froze for just a moment when he saw the robot gliding his way. He felt a hand on his arm and almost yanked it away until he realized it was Tina.

"Yana says we should hide. Let's find an open door." She dragged him over to the wall, and they started touching lights.

"Ugh! Where are we?" Bobcat opened his eyes with a loud groan.

"Hi, sleepyhead. Nice of you to join us." William held out his hand.

"What happened? Did we find the kids?" Bobcat started to look around.

"We were grabbed by some sort of tractor beam or field, at least according to brainiac over there." William pointed to Marcus standing in front of a lander.

"The kids were here at some point, but are gone now. Where here is… is the question of the hour. Look up." William pointed with a raised thumb.

Seeing the glowing green light above them, Bobcat looked toward Marcus and saw all the scrap around them. "What…"

William shook his head. "No idea. Marcus didn't say. Let me show you something."

The LRV known as Rota-Ree sat amidst the wreckage around them. At first glance, it looked beat up but the same. "Under here." William bent down to peer under it.

"They have wired in more LRV batteries along with some I don't recognize. They are even charging in this light. If it could get topside, this thing might make it back to base."

"So, the kids are here then, somewhere… What is all this junk?" Bobcat stared at the lander in front of them.

"That is an LK Soviet Lunar lander." Marcus finally said.

"I thought the Soviets never made it to the moon?" Bobcat asked.

"They didn't. Or at least we at NASA never found proof they did. Some of this other stuff is probes and drones. That is Luna 15. It should be here. The rest?" Marcus shook his head.

"Can we use any of it to get out?"

"Possibly. The children got out somehow. There are drag marks over there as well as a robot of some sort. The damage looks fresh." Marcus walked over to the large, black, mechanical being. He looked over the device and attempted to pry open an access plate.

"Marcus watch out! That thing just moved!" William dropped the probe he was holding and charged over to his friend.

Marcus turned toward William, "What did you say?" He stumbled back falling as the robot suddenly came to life. It began crawling toward the central column's wall.

William helped Marcus stand up and pulled out his ever-present machete.

Marcus grabbed his arm. "Don't. It might lead us to the children."

All three of them watched as the big black robot slowly dragged itself toward the column that dominated the center of the deep crater. The thing must have sent a signal because there was a flash of light and a set of doors opened in the smooth rock wall.

"Do you think that is where the kids went?" Bobcat asked Marcus. All he could think about was John Grimes beating the living crap out of him if he didn't find them.

"It looks like a good place to continue looking." He stepped over the robot entering the small room.

"What about that?" Bobcat pointed at the robot.

William slammed a very large rock onto its head crushing it. "What about it?"

"Why? It may have led us to the children." Marcus glared at William.

"Or it could have signaled other robots to attack us. It's better off dead." William stepped into the white room just as the doors closed behind him.

A door opened, and all five of the students ran inside heedless of what might be there.

"Did it see us?" Tina whispered to Ron.

"I don't think so. I have no idea…" His last words slowly trickled from his mouth as he took in the room.

The lights in the room came on as they entered revealing a freak show of robots and technology. Robotic eyes looked out at them from all over the room. A faint buzzing sound permeated the room suddenly.

Maxim and Nestor squinted as the ultrasonic sound created a sharp pain in their heads. Their enhanced hearing was a liability here.

"Maxim! What's wrong?" Maxim closed his eyes and grabbed the outside of his helmet.

Tina grabbed his arm and pulled him down to her level. "Does your head hurt? Is it the sound?" He nodded his head.

"The helmets only enhance your hearing. Shut them down, and it should block out the sound." She pointed to the controls on her own helmet.

Maxim gave a nod and stuck his tongue out at her, triggering the volume controls. As the sound faded, he opened his eyes and sighed in relief. "What was that?"

"What? Did you say something?" Tina shook her head at him and motioned.

Ron stepped in front of his friend and motioned to him. They touched helmets, and Ron could make himself heard. "There is a speaker mode on the helmets. The toggle for it is in the direction of your left ear. It won't help your ears, but we will be able to hear you."

Both boys looked funny while they tried to turn on the speakers, but were finally able to be heard. "Can you hear us now?" Everyone signaled that they could hear them.

"Ron, can you figure out what is making the noise?" Yana pointed at the dozens of robot heads that were now watching them.

"This tech is beyond me. It would take someone like Marcus to figure it out, but I can try." He approached the work table and began to examine one of the heads.

"Tina, get the boys to help you block the door we came in." Yana pointed to another entrance. "I think we can use that to get out."

The door in question was surrounded by robot bodies and other parts. Not as strong as the Weres, Yana dragged and pushed to move the large items. Across the room, Maxim and Nestor piled machinery and strange looking furniture in front of the door.

"Where do you need me, Yana?" Tina started helping Yana move things.

"Can you help Ron? I'm praying the sound bothering the boys isn't a cry for help from these things."

"Sure. Yana, don't hurt yourself with this. Maxim will be done in a moment." Tina ran to help Ron.

The controls for the door weren't the same as those outside. These seemed like an older design. There were four buttons in a circle, surrounded by lights at each position. Assuming that universally up was up, she pressed the button.

A loud noise sounded, and the door opened. Yana carefully looked through the door. There wasn't a floor! She whirled to tell her friends and came face-to-face with Maxim.

"Can we get out that way?" Maxim boomed with his speaker.

Yana held up her hands in a stop motion. She then pointed at the floor waving them in a 'no-go' signaling motion.

"No floor?" At her nod, he stepped forward and carefully looked up, then down.

"A disposal chute maybe? There might be a way onto other floors." Gripping the side of the door, he leaned out again looking for an interior door control or something.

"We're going to need a long rope or cable."

"Did you find something?" She grabbed his arm and placed her helmet next to his and repeated the question.

"Sort of. There are places on the wall to put feet or hands, but they are short." Maxim held out his hands in a half-foot distance.

"I think we can climb down, but we need to secure to something in case we fall. Not sure how to operate the doors from the inside. Maybe Ron knows how we can find a rope."

"Maxim! I need you!" Nestor's voice boomed out of his speaker as the outer door slid open revealing dozens of large black robots!

Maxim jerked his head up and ran for the door. He grabbed a loose Robot arm from a stack of them as he went past.

"They come!" Nestor shouted and pointed at the now open door.

"Ron, have you found out how to stop the hum?" Yana approached the main entrance with the intent of providing back-up to the others. She now had a robot arm in each hand.

"Neither of us can find anything. It's coming from the heads as far as we can tell." He looked at Tina, and she could only shake her head.

"Then destroy them! We need Maxim and Nestor at their best. Look for rope or wire, something to provide support. We may have to climb out of here." Swinging one of the arms as a club she began pounding on any set of eyes she could find.

Maxim felt the buzzing in his head lessen. He paused from the battle line and carefully turned the volume up on his helmet again.

"…Yana, there are only a couple left. Why did you need rope? All this place has is robot parts!"

Maxim smiled, he could hear again! His voice broke through the mesh of other voices, and he took control once more. "Ron. There is a ladder in the disposal tube. It goes down. We need a way to traverse the tube without dying. The steps are very narrow."

He picked up the now heavily damaged arm and returned to bashing the robots trying to get in. The numbers outside were increasing.

Ron replied, "Maxim, we can use the magnets in our boots to hold onto the wall. I'm going to try it now with Yana holding on to me."

Maxim swung at one of the undamaged robots and almost took its head off with a loud *clang!* "Be careful Tovarich, you are too good a friend to lose. Just be very careful, Ron, and listen to Yana."

Moving around to Nestor's side, Maxim tapped his cousin on the arm and almost lost his own head. Nestor's club came around in a robot-smashing-swing that would have killed someone with lesser reflexes. Maxim ducked and held up his hands.

"Sorry. I thought you were one of them!" He turned and bashed another robot.

Maxim tapped him again, this time tapping his helmet. Quickly touching helmets, he filled his cousin in on what had happened. Nestor dropped out to fix his communications while Maxim took his place.

"Can you hear me now?" Nestor looked back at his cousin.

"Yes, Nestor, I can hear you. Come, let us teach these robots not to mess with the Etheric Academy's Alpha Team!" The two resumed their own private war against the machines.

"Yana, if you and Tina can hold me, I'll try grabbing on with my boots. If the tube isn't magnetic, I might fall, so hold me tight." Ron stepped out into the tube onto the very narrow ledge. Yana grasped his arm and shoulder while Tina held onto Yana. Both had engaged their boots and were anchored to the floor.

Using his left hand, he gripped the wall and put a foot into the small ladder hole. His boots gripped the wall just like the floor. Success! "It worked. I'm going to go down and see if I can get in using the door controls. You can let go of me now."

Ron carefully worked his way down a level to the next door. The outside lock was similar to the one on the above door. He began to try different combinations of lights and directions to 'pick' the lock.

"Maxim, we are losing the door!" Nestor said in a strained voice. More and more robots were flooding in. The robots in the rear were pushing harder and harder in the doorway. The two could hardly keep up under the weight of the onslaught.

"Yana! We are losing! Is there a way out, or do we fight to the death here?" He gave another mighty swing and crushed a head.

"Ron, we have to go. Have you gotten it yet?" Tina peered over the edge. She could see Ron hanging onto a similar ledge trying to get in.

"I've almost got it. There!" The door opened an inch and froze. "Dang it! Give me a minute. I can do this," Ron called back.

Tina looked behind her before looking back at Ron, "We don't *have* a minute. Come on Ron, I know you can do it."

Buoyed by the fact his friends trusted him, he quickly reentered the light code and the door opened. "Woohoo! I got it. Tell everyone to come down."

Tina relayed the message before carefully climbing down herself. Yana was right behind her.

"Time to go, cousin!" Maxim gave a final whack before grabbing his cousin's arm.

The two boys ran for the opening and quickly locked

their boots onto the small, for them, ladder. Back at the door the robots charged again, pushing through the barricade and swarming into the room. The lead robots saw the open door and charged straight ahead, flying out into the void and dropping into the distant incinerator. Many of the others packed into the small space, accidentally pushing several smaller robots out the door. The exterior door finally closed leaving the hallway filled with beaten and battered robots and parts.

CHAPTER FOURTEEN

The elevator containing the BMW crew finally stopped its descent, and the doors opened up. William, brandishing his machete, stepped out. "It's an empty hallway or tunnel thing." The large man stared up at the ceiling and walls as if remembering something.

"Interesting. The construction resembles that of Earth science fiction television. Could there be aliens living among us?" Marcus stared at the ceiling and walls.

"That's why this looks familiar! *Star Journey*! I loved that show as a kid. The sequels sucked." William poked at the wall with his machete.

Bobcat exited last, and the doors slid shut. "Hey! How are we supposed to get back?"

"There are controls on the wall for it, Bobcat. William, look up ahead." Marcus pointed down the hall. Dark shapes littered the hallway ahead. As the three men drew closer, they could see broken and battered robots. A couple of them still moved just a little.

William picked up what looked like a robot arm and gave it a few practice swings. He then proceeded to finish off the robots.

"Why in the hell do you keep doing that?" Marcus glared at the much larger man.

"To keep these things from calling for help. Something obviously thinks they are dangerous."

"They might be friendly. It could be an enemy that is smashing them."

"Marcus, do you truly believe that? Better to ask for forgiveness. If they are friendly, I will apologize after the fact."

Bobcat carefully examined the door and the blinking door controls. "This looks pretty easy. Do you want to go in?"

"Well, the kids might be in there. It's conceivable that all this damage was caused by them. If we open the door, there might be…" William never had a chance to finish his thought. Bobcat heard the words 'open the door' and pressed the button.

An ear-splitting whine was followed by an almost endless stream of large black robots as the door opened. William stared in shock for just a moment before bringing the weapon in his hand to bear.

All three men began pounding on the alien robots. Each of them was much stronger than they appeared. The health benefits of the Queen's plasma and nanocytes had already been proven. Its effects on these men were of restoration and healing. Their slightly enhanced strength was brought to bear against the robots.

"Why," he asked as he hit one robot, "are these things," he swung the opposite direction, "so angry?" He swung his damaged robot arm like a weapon at the attackers.

Marcus, backed up against the wall, was striking out at their eyes and heads. "Maybe they didn't want to be disturbed?"

William was completely surrounded. For each robot he smashed, two more took their place. He was like a threshing machine swinging a robot arm in each hand. "It's your fault Bobcat! Maybe we should start calling you Bozo!"

"That's not fair, and you know it! I just want to find the kids," he grated out.

"You need to add, before John kills you, to that statement." The stream of robots started to slow. Marcus was able to push off from the wall and make his way to William's side.

"I think that may be all of them." William smashed the head of the last robot to come out the door. Piles of broken and blind robots lay all around the big man.

Bobcat began finishing off the few survivors on his side of the hallway. Giving William the benefit of the doubt, Marcus did the same. William carefully climbed over the pile of robots blocking the door and stood up inside the room.

He looked around for a moment and shook his head. "I know why the robots were so angry."

Marcus and Bobcat leaned into the door. "What did you find?

William pointed around the room, "See for yourself, Marcus. The kids have definitely been here."

The other men climbed over the robots and stumbled into the room. All around them were robot heads and a pile of parts. Each of the heads was smashed or ripped to pieces.

Marcus nodded his head. "So, the robots chased them into this room. The heads were destroyed in the battle?"

"If they were chased in here, where are they now? There

were a whole lot of robots in this room!" Bobcat started looking for hidden kids.

"They may have gone out here." William stood next to a small open door surrounded by large robot parts.

Bobcat ran over and jerked the door open. "Whoa!" William had grabbed the smaller man before he took a header out into nothing.

Looking down he saw flames at the bottom of a long shaft. "It's an incinerator tube."

William pulled him back inside and peered in himself. "There is a small ladder leading down the shaft. I think they went down there."

Maxim brought up the rear in their escape from the robot horde. Using his boots, he carefully climbed down the tiny ladder to the floor below. Initially, several of the robots followed him out and nearly hit him on their way down.

"Stupid." He was still muttering the word as he climbed in the small doorway to join his team.

"Why has there been no communica…" Maxim's voice trailed off he was so stunned. The room he entered was only semi-lit. Huge tanks of some form of fluid hung from the ceiling. Each contained what appeared to be a scientific experiment. His four teammates were in front of the last tank.

"Nestor, what is happening?" He laid a hand on his cousin's shoulder.

Yana turned to him with tears in her eyes. "We've found him. He never escaped."

She ran to him and buried her face in his chest. Maxim could only stare at his friends as he held Yana in his arms,

PAUL AND ANDERLE

"What does she mean?"

"It's Andrei Mikoyan. We think he's dead in there." Ron hooked a thumb over his shoulder in the direction of the tanks.

Carefully, Maxim moved the now weeping older girl and passed her to his cousin. "Show me."

The tanks were at least ten feet high. Inside the first was what appeared to be a tabby cat. Around its neck was a striped collar that read 'Flamengo,' beside it was a tiny flag for the country of Brazil. A human floated in the second tank. He was still dressed in spacesuit undergarments from the last century. His features were obscured by damage to his upper body. The third and fourth tanks also contained humans.

"Which one is he?" Ron pointed to the last tank.

The man inside was of medium build with dark hair. His hands bore many wounds, some appeared to be defensive in nature. Maxim could only imagine going up against those robots alone without aid. On his upper shoulder were the letters VDV and a laurel surrounding a torch with wings. It was the symbol of the Russian airborne forces. His grandfather had the same symbol on his shoulder. Unlike the other bodies, this man was definitely Russian.

Not a very religious man, Maxim bowed his head anyway and said a small prayer.

"Is this all there is in here?" He looked at the others.

"No. We found the spacesuits and other gear over there." Tina pointed to the rear of the room. "The other men were US astronauts. The suits say Apollo 20 on them. The guy missing most of his head was a Nazi. He has a swastika on his shoulder and a number on the underside of his left arm. Ron says that is his blood group. He was in the SS." She handed him a patch depicting a lander lifting what looked like an alien spaceship and the words Apollo 20.

"Ron?"

"It shouldn't exist, Maxim. There was a video once about Apollo 20, but is was proven to be a hoax."

"Has anyone checked the door yet?" Maxim pointed to the front of the room.

Ron answered, "We have. It leads to more halls. I told them I wanted to wait for you. If we are attacked again, I can't fight them alone."

Maxim smiled at his friend, "You don't want the glory?"

"No. I wish to survive this. Ending up in a tank like that would be a disgrace to both the training and our team. We will escape this. We will live to tell the world of this man's bravery."

"Would you really do that, Ron? Tell the world, no matter the consequences?" Yana looked up from Nestor's shoulder.

"I would. The Queen respects bravery and sacrifice. Didn't this man sacrifice it all for his country? History makes a mockery of his name. He should be remembered."

Maxim looked down at Ron and smiled. "When we escape, we will shout his name to the heavens. Now, let's get out of here first. Do we have weapons?" He hefted the broken robot arm, "My club is a bit worn out."

"The astronauts had some tools with them as well as… Well, it's a pry bar of some sort." Ron held up what looked like a pry bar from any hardware store on the planet. Only this one was all shiny and had the word NASA on the side of it.

"Handy to have. Is there more?" Maxim asked.

Ron shrugged, "No. Not that I can find."

Maxim thought about it a moment while everyone leaned against something. "Give that to Nestor, Ron. I will use my arm here. It is a tried and true weapon. Give the tools to the girls and stay loose. If I find a gun, I will provide it for you." He looked around after a couple of minutes, "Time to go. Everyone had a chance to eat if you are hungry? Drink too?" They all nodded. "Good, let's move on. Much to see and a way out to find. Someone built all of this. It cannot just be robots."

Maxim waved the rest forward as they exited the room, he paused to give Andrei a final wave.

"Are you sure they went down there?" Marcus looked down the tube a second time.

"It's the only logical way, Marcus. Why am I the one telling you this anyway? Aren't you the brain here?" William stared in amazement at his friend.

"Just playing devil's advocate. How far down do you think they went and how did they open the door to get in?"

William answered, "Does it look like I know the answer to any of that? I was just going to climb down and try picking the door."

"Why don't you take a look at this door first and see if you understand it before charging away down there. OK, William?"

William nodded and sat on the floor just inside the doorway. Sitting like this made it easy to see the door lock and not fall off the edge at the same time.

"Marcus, can you come here a moment?" Bobcat stood next to what looked like a repair station. He was examining the heads that seemed to decorate the room.

"These things are all linked." Bobcat pulled a head off of

the stand, and it made a clicking noise as it separated. The base was like a charging station.

"When the kids came in here, the heads must have told the others where they were. It might be an explanation of how they were all smashed. I think they were all AIs or computer controlled. We need to find the central computer or system command and shut it down."

"That makes sense, which is kind of strange coming from you, Bobcat. I have William figuring out the locking system of the tube. We think the kids went down."

"Why are we going out that way? We didn't see any other robots out in the hall, so we can go that way. There has to be another way down beside the elevator. We even know how to open that, too."

Marcus almost popped himself in the head. He wasn't thinking logically, again. "William! We will try another way down."

"But I think I understand how it works!" he called back.

"Save it. We might need it another time. We'll go out the front." Bobcat opened the front door and looked out. The coast looked clear. "Come on."

CHAPTER FIFTEEN

The hallway outside, what the kids were calling the 'room of horrors,' was different than the one above.

"Did anyone notice the way the hall appears here?" Ron looked up and then down the corridor. "The colors are different, and the pattern on the wall is strange."

Nestor looked up and shook his head. "Not much of one. It might just be from construction. Let's check out the other rooms."

The cousins took the lead for opening doors. Nestor held his club at the ready while Maxim tried the lock. Pressing multiple combinations didn't work like before, but the NASA crowbar they found worked just fine.

"Why does this feel wrong to me?" Tina watched down the hall as Maxim pried the door open.

Yana was watching the opposite hall, "Too many episodes of Cops and Robbers on that idiot box you Americans call television."

Tina thought about that, "That may be true. My little brother, Todd, likes all those shows. What do you think is in there?" Tina nodded her head toward the room.

"I am hoping there are no more glass tubes. I... I am not over seeing the body of Andrei. No one should be displayed as such. His last words in the log will scar me for life. My father has tried to get me to see what you call the 'Big Picture.' I see now what he was trying to tell me. The Queen is right in many things. Injustice must be fought."

Tina laughed. "Philosophical discussions while running from killer alien robots. You are truly the best of friends." She gave Yana a quick hug.

There was a loud crunch, and the sound of tearing metal, and the door finally opened. "I did it!" Maxim smiled at his cousin.

Both cousins threw their weight at it, and the door opened with a *bang!* Everyone rushed into the room with weapons held high. The automatic lights came up revealing a room filled with blinking lights and monitors.

"No robots!" Nestor put his club down in disgust.

"Did you want more trouble?" Maxim gave his cousin a little push.

"Sort of? Just wanted to get my mad out on something. What is this place?" Nestor peered at a blinking machine.

"Looks like a control room of some kind." Ron started pressing buttons and watching the screens for results.

"Ron, be careful you don't blow us all up!" Yana stepped over and peered at the monitors with him.

Ron looked at her with an almost maniacal grin. "What is the worst that could happen? More robots?"

"Or a self-destruct device. Be careful."

Ron put his hand over his heart, "OK. I promise not to

blow us up." Yana snorted and moved to examine another piece of equipment.

Suddenly a three-dimensional image appeared in the center of the room. It showed a hallway and then changed to a different one.

"Ron? Is that the security system?" Maxim stared at the flashing images.

"It might be. This panel is broken up into five sections. These might be floors or different base divisions. Without signs or descriptions, I can't tell. It sort of looks like the holo-pad from the *Battle Stars* movie series. Remember when the Darth is talking to the Emperor?"

"I've never seen that show before. Wait, stop! Go back." Maxim stared intently at the flickering screen.

"You've never seen *Battle Stars*? Have you been living under a rock? What are we searching for here?" Ron's fingers flashed on the control panel as he worked his way back through the buttons.

"There! Freeze it right there."

"What is it?" Ron stopped and stepped over to the center of the room. He and the others gasped at what they saw.

Team BMW was standing in a hallway battling the big black robots the kids were running from. As they watched, William bashed away at them with a robot arm.

Nestor stared down at his own makeshift club and smiled. "How did they get here?"

"The same as us, I bet. They must have come looking for us." Tina leaned in closer to the image.

Marcus and Bobcat were each battling robots, catching those that got away from William.

"That is the room we escaped from!" Yana pointed out the smashed robot heads.

"We should go back and find them."

"Tina, I don't think that is a good idea." Yana looked at her smaller friend.

"I don't see why not, Yana. There haven't been any more robots in the halls."

"Did you mean like those?" Ron pointed at a couple of the larger ones watching the adult men enter the parts room. The robots glided to a stop outside of the room, appeared to look in, then went off in a different direction.

"Can you track where they went?" Nestor pointed at the control board in front of the boy.

"I can try." Ron started pressing buttons again as he searched for the robots.

Multiple images flashed on the screen from what appeared to be the same floor. As Ron pressed the last button in the sequence, the group could see their quarry enter one of the elevators and go somewhere else.

"Does the elevator have a camera in it?" Maxim stared at the images.

"You're asking me? I have no idea." Ron scanned the panel trying to understand the patterns and symbols.

"Guys, check this out," Tina called the others over.

Yana peered over her shoulder and gasped. "Where is that?"

"What is that, you mean?" Maxim stared at an image of a room filled with what looked like sleeping aliens.

The aliens looked like they were shorter than humans. It was hard to tell from the screen.

"Are they dead, or just sleeping?" Nestor looked at Tina.

"I think this monitors them. See here on the panel? That looks like some sort of biofeedback." Tina ran her hand down a blinking panel showing the older boy.

"We need to stay away from there. Robots are one thing,

but actual aliens could be worse. They think different. Look for a way out that doesn't involve waking them up." Yana snapped out the last bit like an order. Maxim started at her tone, but nodded.

Live aliens were an unknown element.

"I think I see a possible way out. There is another one of those elevators on this level. Or at least I think it's this level. The wall patterns match this one." Ron pointed.

"Someone leave a message for Marcus. If they are following us, they should know where we went."

"But Yana, shouldn't we just stay here and wait for them?" Tina protested.

"They may be attacked by robots again. We have nowhere to run to if they chase them here to us. We need someplace defensible or to escape to. I agree with Yana. We must think defensively." Maxim turned toward Tina.

"But… He's my friend. I want to help them."

"We are your friends, too, Tina. Marcus and the guys would want you to survive. We need to stick together in this." Maxim studied the smaller girl.

Tina bit her lip, then nodded, "OK. Let's go then."

"Well, that sucked." Bobcat stared at the blank wall and frowned. "You would think there would be a door or a stairwell right here. It only makes sense."

"Alien minds are alien. You have to remember that, Bobcat." Marcus looked away from him and stared back the way they came.

"Did you read that on the back of a cereal box or something?" Bobcat asked.

The three adults had followed the sloping floor down two levels. Similar in design to an Earth parking garage, they had discovered that all levels were connected until now.

"Are we sure there is even another level down? We tried going up, and that was blocked, too. Maybe the elevator is all there is to get out." William pointed up.

"William, how many levels down did you count in the tube?" Marcus tried one of the door controls again. So far, he had been able to open several using an arithmetico-geometric sequence.

Cocking his head to one side, William thought for a moment, "I remember four for sure. Maybe five if you count the very bottom."

"That's what I thought. We have come down only two. Not knowing what level the kids are on is maddening, but if we find the way out, one of us can search for them."

"One of us? You might as well just say *William will look for them*. Neither one of us is strong enough to take on a bunch of robots alone. William over there has a double boost." Bobcat flicked his wrist and thumb at his tall friend.

"A double boost? I'm afraid to ask, but what does that mean?" William glared at his friend.

"You have some of The Queen's blood in you as well as Akio's. They both gave you some." Bobcat smiled, but he wiggled his eyebrows like one of the Marx brothers while doing it.

"That does not count, and you know it! He only gave me his blood to save my life!" William paused and cocked his head before looking back at Bobcat, "He's like my blood brother now."

"Is that all he is to you?" Bobcat smiled, he really loved getting this man all riled up.

"Stop it you two, or I'll stop the car! I swear if you are going to act like children I'll start treating you like it." Marcus threw up his hands in exasperation. Bobcat looked over at William and stuck out his tongue.

Shaking his head, Marcus tried another door. He looked back over his shoulder. "Start thinking about which way you wish to try. One level or two as we backtrack."

The door opened while he was still talking and he was pulled suddenly into the room!

The lights came up as Marcus tried to fight the very large robot arm that had grabbed his hand. It was at least twice the size of the smaller units William had been smashing.

He felt himself being thrown down to the floor and hit with some sort of immobilizing ray. He could only watch as his friends, his brothers from other mothers that he both loved and respected, battle the monster.

Bobcat and William watched as their friend fell or was pulled into the room he was opening.

"Marcus!" Bobcat yelled after him.

William was closer and made it to the door before it closed. The sight of his friend lying dead or dying on the floor threw him into a rage. All he could see was red as he began pounding on the giant robot.

Bobcat, trying to stay out of range of the robot, dodged to the right and tried to drag Marcus out of the fight. William was pounding on the robot like a man possessed.

"Marcus? Can you hear me? Tell me a stupid math joke if you can!" Bobcat shook Marcus and tried to see if he was still breathing.

"If you kiss me, I'll punch you," Marcus looked up into Bobcat's eyes.

"Oh, thank the stars! I can't bear to lose another friend."

William ducked as the robot went on the offensive. Its large arms came at him in pincer movements, as well as some sort of ray that slowed his movements.

"Uh, guys, if you're finished making out," he slammed his machete into the robot, "can you give me a hand, please?" The ray made his legs heavy, and he was about to slam into the floor when Bobcat lit into the robot from behind.

"Stop hurting my friend!" Bobcat's blows were aimed at the control panels on the outside of the robot as well as its eyes and sensors.

Landing on his knee, William grimaced, but regained his balance. He swung at his opponent's head and landed a heavy blow that made a loud *clang!*

The robot turned back toward William bringing its arms around again as Bobcat scored a hit on its controls causing it to spin out of control onto the floor. Using his machete as well as the improvised club William finished it off.

"Bigger they are…"

"The harder they fall." Bobcat finished William's sentence for him. They smiled at each other like little kids.

"I bet this guy's head would look good on the wall at All Guns Blazing."

Bobcat looked down at the robot and thought about it a moment before asking, "How would we get it there? It's pretty big."

"I could cut it off." William made a swinging motion with his machete.

Marcus lay on the floor wondering if he should get better friends.

CHAPTER SIXTEEN

These robots might be aliens, but they have some really cool stuff." Bobcat let the strange computer module drop to the floor with a loud *bang!*

"Bobcat, be careful with that!"

"You mean this thing, Marcus?" He dropped another of the modules on top of the other one.

Marcus winced as each one hit the floor, "Yes, that! What we can learn from that, can advance some of our technology by hundreds of years."

"It won't do us any good when we're all dead! That is exactly where we will be if we don't get out of this place!" Bobcat tossed yet another piece of hardware into the pile.

Marcus stared at his friend and shook his head. "Knowledge is always important, and you're wrong," he answered.

"Wrong about what?" Bobcat looked up at him from his growing pile of stuff.

"That the robots are the aliens. A robot didn't build this." Marcus held up a handheld control unit. "Why would they? There are aliens here somewhere."

"He's right. Why would a mechanical being create locks that require buttons? There have to have been aliens with hands here at one point." William held up one of the locking mechanisms.

Bobcat looked around, "Wait, there are aliens in here? With us?"

Marcus looked over at William. "Why does the Queen keep him?"

"He has his uses. Just excuse him today, Marcus. Ever since the kids went missing, he's had a case of the dumbs."

"Hey! I'm right here. Stop talking like I'm not." Bobcat glared at his two supposed friends.

"Are you with us and ready to get out of here now, Bill?" William looked at his old friend.

"That is not my name anymore, and you know it. Bill was a guy just barely making it on his own. I'm not him. I'm the guy who helped build the first pod, who supervised the construction of the Meredith Reynolds and built the best bar this side of Alpha Centauri. Bill is just Bill. I'm Bobcat, the helicopter pilot tapped by Bethany Anne to help her save people from a bank attack." He squared his shoulders, "Let's go kick some alien ass!" He marched out of the room and took a right to go down the hall.

"Wait for it," William said to Marcus.

"Uh, huh."

Bobcat's head reappeared in the doorway a moment later. "Which way is out, do you think?"

His friends busted out laughing.

PAUL AND ANDERLE

✤ ✤ ✤

"What if there is no opening to the outside?" Yana stared up at Maxim's feet.

"Then we try something else. We were looking for something we could defend. Why not take the high ground? Besides, why build a ladder if there is no opening." Maxim paused to take a breath. He wasn't too tired, but the climb was pretty long.

The kids were climbing single-file up the incinerator tube ladder. They knew that the lower floors held more robots as well as aliens and had decided to go up.

"Can…" Pant. "We…" pant. "Stop… for… a moment." Ron all but gasped his sentence out. He wasn't in as good of a shape as the larger boys. Computers and inside activities, preferably ones where he sat down, were more his speed.

Tina looked up at Ron and seconded the motion to the others.

"Cousin, we need to slow down again for the others." Nestor relayed the message.

"OK. Everyone lock your boots to the wall." He reached down and pressed the magnetize button at his waist.

Everyone hung there inside the metallic tube for several minutes. They had already passed the first subterranean floor and were about halfway to the summit.

"Remember when we get there to be careful not to smash anything that looks important. Finding the way out is the most important thing we have to do."

Maxim could see the top of the shaft from where he stood. To him, it looked a bit like a shower head, only upside down. The ceiling was curved and perforated by several holes. Ron and Tina had already speculated that they might be there to release gasses to space. That was something he didn't care in the least about. His entire focus was on the tiny ledge at the very top of the ladder built into the wall. There was a door inset into the wall, and he could just barely see the edge of it.

"Ron, do you want to try to pick it first?"

"That would be a lot quieter, Maxim. I can see if the same code works twice."

"Good. Can you get up here?"

"I can try." Ron stepped off the tiny ladder and engaged his boots to hold him steady as he climbed. Like an old fashioned free climber, he slid past Nestor and Yana, only occasionally touching his friends.

"You do that like you were born to do it. When we get to ship's maintenance class, you're going to smoke all of us. You watch." Maxim took Ron's hand and pulled him closer, steadying him as he stepped back onto the ladder.

"It's easy. You should try it." Ron's cheeks warmed with the praise of his friend.

"You can teach me. But not here. Save it for school when we get home. Now, see if you can open the door."

The younger boy slipped past Maxim and pulled himself onto the tiny ledge. The door looked exactly like those down below in the lower levels. Ron used the combination of lights and finger movements that enabled him to escape the robots. The lock blinked like a strobe for a moment, and the door hissed open.

"Got it!"

"Ron, wait for me to go first." Maxim watched as he opened the door wider and stuck his head inside.

"I don't see anything. No robots or aliens." Ron looked into Maxim's eyes. "Uh, oops?"

"Death wish much, Ron? Go on in, I will bring up the

rear." He pointed toward the door.

"Great!" He pushed the door open the rest of the way and crawled into the darkened room.

Ron stood and peered into the gloom. Small lights blinked across the room casting shadows that danced on the rounded walls of the room.

"Oof! I hate these low doors. Do you see anything?" Maxim half crawled, half stood up in the room.

"Not yet." Ron tapped his helmet, engaging the lights. The visor lights lit up, turning Ron's head into a flashlight. He swung his head left then right, half blinding Maxim in the process.

"Hey! Stop!" Maxim covered his eyes until Ron settled down. "Slowly, look around."

"Sorry." Ron stepped up to the panel containing the lights and examined it.

"Everyone alive in here?" Yana peered into the room.

"So far. I think we're alone. Come on in." Maxim urged the others out of the tube.

Tina was the last to enter, and as she crawled inside, she could have sworn she heard her name. She froze and looked around. "Maxim, did you just call me?"

Puzzled Maxim looked at her. "No, why?"

"I could have sworn I heard my name being called. This place has me all confused. It's not a big deal, don't worry about it."

Maxim frowned and stuck his head out into the tube and looked around. He peered over the edge and couldn't see anything. If only he had waited just a moment longer.

"Are you sure this is going to work?" asked Bobcat for the thirtieth time.

"Yes. It should. Go away. Please?" Marcus scowled at his friend for the fifth or sixth time in a row.

William silently laughed over the whole thing. Between the two of them, they were unable to remove the robot head from its body. They were both still moping over it. Marcus proposed after he got up off the floor, that they hot-wire the elevator they knew about and to get back to the surface at least. They might be able to figure out a way to either call for help, or get the pod to come down. Either was worth a try.

Bobcat was sulking, and Marcus knew it. "Bobcat quit worrying about John killing you and give us a hand. If we can get this dang elevator working, we will have access to what is above us and possibly below. Then all we have to do is find the kids and leave this place." Marcus looked up from the panel he was dismantling.

"Marcus keep working, I have him." William stepped over and patted Bobcat on the back.

"Dude. Leave him alone to work. If he gets it wrong, we could slam into the bottom of the shaft, and all die. Who wants that? I know we didn't get the big robot's head, but I seem to remember a whole bunch of small ones over in that room over there." William pointed to the robot apocalypse room.

"It was them, I swear!" Bobcat stammered to his friends.

William crawled back out of the small doorway and shook his head at Marcus. "Tell us again what it is you think you saw."

"I am not crazy! Most of the robot heads were smashed, so I went over to the door and looked down the tube. I could see what we think is the incinerator at the bottom. So, I looked up. Tina, or someone that looks like her, was all the way at the top of the shaft climbing into the wall. I called her name, but she didn't stop. That's when I got you two." Bobcat pointed at the door.

William looked at Marcus. "If he is telling the truth, and he did see them, is it possible to even climb that tube? I mean, I can barely fit through the door."

Marcus looked at both of them and looked out into the tube again. He carefully reached out and touched the small ladder and walls. Back inside, he replied, "Maybe. They are smaller than us and could, in theory, use the ladder."

Staring at his friend William shook his head. "That's nuts. I've done some stupid stuff before, but climb a tiny ladder up who knows how far?"

Tapping his fingers on one of the smashed robots Marcus looked up to the ceiling in thought. "They might have discovered how to use the mag-boots. The tube is metallic, and the boots would work better than rubber shoes for climbing. It's possible. We, however, cannot go that way."

"Why, the door is right there?" Bobcat practically shouted.

"William cannot fit through the door, and none of us have any practice using the mag-shoes. If one of us falls… Well, you know. The elevator is our best bet. At least we know they are still alive."

Bobcat looked back at the tube, "If you say so, Marcus. I really want to try to go after them."

"Do this. Practice walking in the boots here on this floor. Use the walls and the floor outside in the hall." Marcus pointed.

Bobcat ran out to practice, and William managed to grab him before he fell on his head the very first time.

Bobcat's mouth pressed together, "OK, I see your point. Elevator it is."

CHAPTER SEVENTEEN

I s this another control room?" Yana looked over the massive console of blinking lights.

"I'm not completely sure, but Nestor and I think it's the tractor beam control and the EM field." Ron carefully ran his hands across the panels.

"Look, this section here is the tractor. We are pretty sure because there is a range control as well as automatic." Tina watched as they pointed out the controls.

"OK, so what about the rest of this stuff?" Yana spread her arms about the room.

"It's a ship. Like the flying saucers in the comics I have seen." Everyone looked at Maxim.

"Think about it; it covers the whole crater. It's like a ground spider trap. The underside is lit, and both the elevator and the incinerator tube are attached to the ground. This is how the Aliens that we saw down there move about." Maxim pointed down.

ALPHA CLASS

"Whose ship is it? I mean, we know it's not Kurtherians because I've been told about TOM's ship and it looks nothing like this one." Tina said.

"Tina, are you sure? TOM himself and the Queen have said there are thirteen tribes of Kurtherians. Only seven are bad." Ron stepped closer to her.

Tina shook her head. "I'm pretty sure. This is something else. If we can get out of here, we will be heroes for finding and stopping an alien ship."

Yana was listening to her friends argue over what sort of ship this was and who should take credit while she investigated the controls.

Ron and Nestor were the mechanics of the group, but she was quickly gaining some awareness of how the controls on this ship were laid out. The room they were in was round and central to the craft, if it was a ship they were inside. The control panels appeared to be set in a circle around the center. The walls contained a couple of indented spaces, which might conceal hidden doors. It was the floor that concerned her the most. It looked to be circular and contain something.

"Uh, excuse me?" The others continued to argue over who was right.

"Tina! Would you and Ron stop for a moment? Something isn't right." Yana was on her hands and knees touching a groove in the floor.

The others looked in her direction and stopped arguing. "What is it Yana?"

"This groove is a complete circle, and it's vibrating."

Maxim stepped over to Yana and touched the groove. "Just the circle or the whole floor?"

Yana shook her head. "Just the circle I think. It comes

and goes, but it is almost stuttering like an engine trying to turn over."

Both Ron and Nestor joined them in touching the circle. Tina noticed a new panel that had begun to blink. "Ron, come look at this. Is that the elevator?"

Staring at the panel Ron could see each floor of the base highlighted and a small light moving up and down the column erratically. "It might be. I think the robots are using it to search for us."

"Why is it only moving between floors then?" Tina traced the movement of the light with her finger. At the moment her finger touched the panel, another light lit up. The back and forth motion of the elevator stopped, it was now going straight up.

"Tina, take your hand off the panel! It's touch sensitive." Ron stared in horror at the panel.

"Yana! That circle is the elevator, and it's on its way up! They've found us!" Tina yelled at the others.

"Who found us? The robots?" Maxim stood up and looked at his friends.

"I touched a panel, and the elevator changed direction. It is coming here!" Tina pointed to the light.

"Everyone, grab your weapons and get ready. We will smash the robots as soon as they exit." Maxim and Nestor grabbed their clubs and stood ready.

"This thing is making me sick!" William held his stomach.

Marcus had managed to get the elevator open again. He dismantled the controls and put it in motion at long last. Unfortunately, his command of the alien technology wasn't perfect. The elevator was being erratic moving swiftly in one direction before reversing. It was similar to a yo-yo or carpenter's bubble.

"I'm trying to stabilize the gyroscopic controls, but they keep being overridden by something." Marcus continued to poke and prod at the blinking lights and the attached wires. Then he wiggled the conduits hanging from the control panel causing the elevator to jerk.

"Dude, you need to work faster. If he yacks, it will get both of us in here. What about this one?" Bobcat touched a blinking light, and the elevator juddered to a stop.

Marcus grabbed his friend's hand and pulled him away. "Stop touching things! You are only making it worse."

"How is this worse. We are at least stopped." He glanced at William. "Does that help, buddy?"

William nodded and clutched his stomach. Suddenly the elevator lurched upward.

"Marcus, stop it! William needs to rest a minute." Bobcat glared at the scientist.

"This is not me. I haven't touched a thing here." He pointed to the blinking cables which were all blinking in unison now.

"Could it be robots?" Bobcat picked up Williams club.

"It's possible," Marcus agreed.

Bobcat looked to his friend, "William, are you in any shape to fight?"

William snatched his robot arm from Bobcat's grasp and gave it a few practice swings. "I think I can handle myself."

"What am I supposed to use?" Bobcat looked around the mostly empty elevator.

Marcus pointed to his feet. "You could throw a robot head at them?"

"Nope. These are going on the wall of the bar as trophies. I'll just hide this trophy back behind William." He laid the head behind William and turned around to prepare for any possible attack.

The control panel lights began to dim their blinking as the elevator slowed to a stop. The door opened to a mostly dark room. William could see a dark shape approach the door, and he gave a yell and swung his makeshift club!

Nestor ducked to avoid the club aimed at his head and yelled at his attacker. "Stop! It's us!"

William pulled his back swing and ordered the 'voice' to step into the light. "You almost lost a head there, kid!"

"It's you! Are the rest of the kids with you?" Bobcat stepped around William and confronted Nestor.

"We're here." Tina and the others crowded around the entrance.

"Great. Let us get out of here before it decides to take off on its own again." Marcus pointed to the glowing spaghetti factory hanging from the wall.

"Sir, it shouldn't do that. We have the master control for it over there." Ron hooked a finger over his shoulder.

Marcus looked at the confident young man. "Do you really? What else have you discovered?" The two of them separated from the group and began to examine the control panels.

Yana looked at Bobcat and tried to sound like she wasn't worried. "Mr. Bobcat, Sir? Are we in trouble?"

Bobcat chuckled. "Well, you did find an Alien base and did not die. John Grimes won't need to kill me for his cousin's daughter, and all of you, of course. So, all's right with that world." He jerked a thumb over his shoulder, "We found the robots you left us down there."

Nestor grimaced. "Yeah, sorry about that. They were chasing us."

"We figured that out after seeing the smashed ones. Good work, by-the-way for surviving." William, Maxim, and Nestor looked at each other's robot arm clubs and smiled.

"What else did you find down there?" Bobcat directed his question at Yana.

"Did you see Andrei and the other humans in the tanks?" she asked.

"You found humans?" Marcus spoke from outside the group. He had been listening as Ron showed him the consoles.

"Yes, sir. They were like science experiments in big clear tubes. Russian, American, and what looked like a Nazi were there."

Tina spoke up. "Don't forget the cat, Yana."

"Sorry, yes, there was a tabby cat in the tubes, too." She smiled at Tina.

"Strange. I don't think NASA ever used cats for space launches. You said you found a Nazi? From World War Two, those Nazis?" Marcus stepped away from Ron and approached the group.

"Yes, Marcus. Ron and I found a Nazi rocket down in the junkyard as well as a lot of other things. Did you see the Russian LK lander? We read the pilot's diary."

"Be sure you write down what you remember when we return. The Queen will want a full report on all of this. We will have to explain how you ended up here outside of commands, but I don't think you will be in too much trouble." Bobcat tapped a finger. "Did you see any Aliens or just robots?"

"There is a whole room full of them somewhere down

there," Maxim looked at Bobcat. "We could see them, but couldn't tell where they were."

"You know they could be up here with us. This is a ship." Ron pointed to the walls around them.

"Should we look? I mean there are more of us now." Yana pointed to the voids that just had to be doors to more rooms.

Marcus looked at what she was indicating. He shook his head. "Let's try to find a way out of here first. If that search leads us to them, so be it. But first use the resources here at hand."

Breaking up into groups the students and adults began to examine each control station and define its use.

The elevator was the only thing that went outside the room, but only down to the junkyard.

"If we can get to the surface, do you think our Moon rover has enough juice to get us to safety?" Maxim, Nestor, and William played with the elevator controls.

"Why do we need the LRV?" William touched the screen again bringing the elevator up. It wouldn't go past the second level or up past where they stood.

"To get home. We already souped it up and extended the battery life. We owe those engineers who rebuilt them."

"No, Maxim. You're missing my point. Why do we need one? We left an extra five-passenger Pod in stationary orbit above us. All we have to do is shut down the EM field and get out of here for a pickup." William pointed up.

"Is that why you haven't called it down yet? Should we expect the Queen's Marines or Guard, too?" Tina looked up at the ceiling.

Both Bobcat and William winced. "Uh, this is sort of an off the books rescue. We didn't tell anyone we were coming down here after you. Our LRV was sucked into the EM field just as yours was."

"So, no one is coming for us?" Yana looked up from the controls she was staring at.

William shook his head. "No. Not yet. They will notice we haven't checked in soon, though. Let's just get out of here for now."

"I can't find anything. Let's look in these rooms." Yana stepped up to the void on the wall and began feeling for a control.

"Yana, we aren't ready to…" Marcus called.

Yana must have touched something because a door whooshed open suddenly. Without entering, they could all see it was another small room with even more control panels.

No robots or Aliens were hidden in it.

Marcus shook his head. "Yana, stop using Bobcat as an example. Wait before leaping. Carefully open the other door and get this out of the way."

Tina and Ron were closest to the door and began to feel for a lock. Suddenly, a door opened almost knocking them down as the pressure equalized.

Clubs at the ready, Nestor and Maxim peeked into the room. It, like the other, was empty. It did, however, have what appeared to be an airlock in the wall.

"This looks promising Marcus," Nestor called out from the doorway.

Marcus examined the airlock on the wall and smiled. "This looks to be an escape hatch. We won't know until it opens, but it may be a way out."

"Are you sure?" Bobcat stared at the obviously Alien portal.

"It's the best option we've found so far." Marcus examined the door switch.

"What about this control panel Marcus?" Tina looked over

at the smiling rocket scientist.

"It could be anything. Ignore it for now. When we return, we will examine everything. Get the others. It's time to go."

Tina ran to get the others together.

Bobcat dropped the trio of robot heads he was dragging around on the deck of the ship. "Let's get this show on the road. I have a dinner date to make and a girl to woo."

William nudged his friend and laughed. "A date? Woo hoo! Fancy. Where are you taking her?"

Bobcat blushed. "Not sure yet. Australia maybe? I need to ask some of the girls for advice."

"Well, you could take her to that little place we went to in Melbourne. It was nice." Bobcat nodded his head in agreement.

"Not to intrude upon your discussion, but it's time to go." Marcus gave his two friends a hard stare.

"Oops. Sorry. Are the kids ready?" Bobcat looked around and found them staring at him.

Marcus pressed several of the controls and the door irised open. He peeked inside. "It's a pressure chamber to the outside. This is it."

Not worrying about pressure, Marcus opened the outer door. There was a rush of the atmosphere as the pressures equalized. The surface of the moon could be seen outside.

Marcus looked at the line of students. Tina was last in line. "Tina, do me a favor and turn off the EM field. It will help us to call down the pod." She ran back to the other room.

"William will go first, followed by all of the students. Bobcat and I will bring up the rear. When you get outside, get clear of the ship and out onto the surface of the moon. We cannot be sure if we will be pursued or not." Marcus pointed to William.

As the others departed, Bobcat spoke to Marcus. "Do you think we will be chased? The kids did say they saw Aliens."

"I'm just being careful. There might be more robots or a failsafe. Just watching out for our charges."

Tina came rushing back. "I turned off the EM, Marcus."

"Excellent. Go join the others."

Tina smiled and ran for the door. Not seeing Bobcat's robot heads on the floor, she tripped over them. Her momentum combined with the half gravity caused her to glide rather than fall, and she crashed headlong into the lone control panel in the room.

Marcus, worried, rushed over to her, "Tina are you alright?"

She steadied herself on the floor and grabbed the control panel as she pulled herself up. "I…I think so."

"Careful don't touch the panel control!" Marcus could only watch as her hand brushed the control activating it.

Bobcat replied for him. "Too late."

Lights in the room began to flash. An Alien voice began to speak. The tones and grunts being spoken reminded Marcus of the noises seals or walruses make.

"What did I do?" Tina looked, eyes open wide, at the panel she touched.

"Not sure." Marcus bent down and examined the now violently blinking panel. The tones being spoken were now coming faster and more hurried.

"Sounds like a countdown." Bobcat cocked his head and stared at the ceiling.

"Tina, go ahead and join your friends." They watched as she ran out the door.

"Self-destruct maybe? It's in the right place for it," Marcus commented.

"You are such a downer, Marcus! We should leave, shouldn't we?" Bobcat asked as the two men started towards the exit.

PAUL and ANDERLE

"Ya think?" The two of them ran out the portal and jumped off the ship's side. The others were milling around on the top edge of the crater and could only stare at them.

Everyone felt a rumbling as what felt like successive explosions rocked the Alien base. There was a brilliant flash of blue light that enveloped the entire area for just a moment then went away. The ship they had all just left, dropped down and crashed into the bottom of the hole, as the elevator shaft collapsed.

Tina looked at Marcus, tears were running down her face. "I'm so sorry."

"It's not your fault, Tina. If anyone is to blame for this, it's Bobcat for leaving those robot heads where someone could trip over them," he told her.

"My heads! I left them!" Bobcat turned toward Marcus and pointed, "I blame you for this."

CHAPTER EIGHTEEN

Bobcat looked over the edge of the crater and mumbled, "My heads."

"You and your heads. We still have the arms!" William held up the pair of robot arms they had been using as clubs.

"Those are not as cool as robot heads. Maybe we can go down and look for them later. What do you think, Marcus?" Bobcat looked at his friend.

"The technology is impressive. Maybe we can salvage it later after we tell the Queen it was destroyed."

"Crap! I forgot about that part. She's going to be pissed, isn't she? We didn't tell her about the search or anything did we?" Bobcat's eyes were now very wide.

"No, we didn't. What do we do? You've known her longer than we have." William looked at his friend.

"Who, me? She hired me, then you. Don't give me that

crap. We are all so dead." Bobcat looked over at the students. They were clustered near the crater talking.

"We could blame the kids, but those two sisters would still come after me. What if we pretend that nothing happened? No alien base or ship. We tell the kids not to say anything." William looked to Marcus.

"She would still catch us. You have both told me yourselves that the Queen reads minds."

"That's true, but she doesn't do that to her friends, Marcus. William's idea might work." Bobcat jumped in.

William called the kids over to the discussion. "We have a minor problem. No one but us knows about what happened down there. We would like to make a bargain with you. Forget that the ship and base exist, and we will ignore your trip out of bounds and disobeying orders."

"Hide it from the Queen? Doesn't she read minds and stuff?" Tina could only stare.

"She doesn't do that to friends. We will tell her about what happened eventually, just not right now. She doesn't need to know we almost got all of you killed. Clean slate."

The kids looked at their smiling mentors and started to discuss it.

"Ya think they will go for it?" Bobcat looked to William.

"They should. It will leak, though. Those kids can't be trusted not to talk about the cool stuff on the moon. I just hope the Queen isn't too mad at us about it." William looked down at his feet.

"The Pods are on their way down. I called in the extra one. There are more than five of us here. The E.I. told me that only the Academy has inquired about the moon. You two may have gotten away with this escapade." Marcus walked over holding his tablet.

"Us? Marcus, we are all in this together." Bobcat looked at his friend.

Marcus smiled, "I will just say I was coerced. Have they decided to lie for you?"

"Not yet. William was just going to ask them." Bobcat gave his friend a little shove.

"Me?" William turned back and made faces at his friends. "What's the verdict kids?"

Maxim and Yana turned away from the others and looked at him. "You are going to tell the Queen about this?"

"We intend to, yes."

"Then you have a deal. We won't say anything to the other classes or to the Ds for two weeks. Does that work for you?"

William nodded. "I'll tell them, but it works. The Pods are on the way, so get ready to leave."

William walked back to where Marcus and Bobcat were standing. "They are giving us a couple of weeks to fess up to the Queen, but they will keep quiet until then."

"Score!" Bobcat made a fist pump motion.

Marcus shook his head. "Less trouble if we fess up now. Whatever. Let's get out of here."

Silently, the two pods dropped out of the sky and hovered several feet off the surface of the moon.

"Our ride's here. Everyone get on board one of them." William pointed at the prototype Pods.

Bobcat and Marcus took off with half the kids while William took the other half. First stop was the mostly dismantled TQB base. The hanger bay retracted and the pods entered. As the doors to the bay closed and re-pressurized, Marcus talked to the students.

"You have two weeks left with us. How would you like to help us build the next stage of Pod development up on the Meredith Reynolds? Or we can stay down here and pack some more."

The overall choice was to go back to the asteroid base. The promise of hot food, showers, and a normal, robot free schedule appealed to the kids more than packing up a moon base.

"How are we going to get this job done down here? We don't have all that much time. I promised Jean she could destroy it." Bobcat looked all around as the kids jumped off the pods.

"We've already taken the important stuff off the base. Why not let her do it? You're just being too picky." William gave Bobcat a look.

"Fine. Whatever. Let's get our stuff so I can get out of this space suit and into something more comfortable."

"He really does need a girlfriend. I hope this new girl can handle his moodiness." William remarked to Marcus.

"It's my understanding she's Wechselbalg. She can do it." Looking around and sniffing, Marcus looked back at William. "He has a point. Let's get out of these suits."

When everyone was reasonably clean and odor free, they gathered in the makeshift cafeteria. One thing the spacesuit designers had not yet mastered was scent elimination. The orbital miners had their own decontamination areas that were upwind of the regular ones, for obvious reasons.

"It's too bad the base was destroyed, but did we gain any knowledge from its destruction?" Bobcat sat at the head table.

Ron jumped up to answer. "Both NASA and the Soviets had secret space programs that put people on the moon."

"Very good, Ron. Yes, some of what we found was rumored when I worked for NASA, but not to this extent. It was unfortunate about the Soviet attempts. Our current government is a mess, as some of you are already aware. When we tell the Queen about our adventure, we will share the story you learned about. Contacting a country's government is her job, not ours. What else did we learn?"

"Alien robots are not to be discounted," Maxim answered from the front row.

"I can agree to that one. Some of those were really tough." William nodded to the boy.

Tina raised her hand. "Will the Queen be mad the base was destroyed?"

"Maybe. However, she will be upset with us, not you. Tina, what happened is none of your fault. We," Marcus pointed at Bobcat and William. "Should have called in the Marines instead of searching for you ourselves. That is on us. Depriving the world of destructive tech is one of our goals, so in that we are safe. She likes us too much. Don't worry."

Bobcat leaned close to William and whispered. "I'm worried."

Maxim and Nestor both smirked and coughed loudly to remind the adults that they could hear everything. Bobcat winked to the two of them, he hadn't forgotten.

Marcus spoke up, "Finish your food and get your kits together. The Pods leave in an hour." All of the kids dropped their food in the trash and headed back to their room to pack.

William looked down at his meal in a bag. "It doesn't taste all that bad, does it? Reminds me of boot camp."

"Only you, William. This stuff tastes like boot heel. I know they keep trying to make it better, but they have yet to succeed. The suit food is better than this stuff." Bobcat tossed his pouch in the trash with the others.

Marcus continued to eat after the others left. He was an

academic and had been very poor most of his life. Food was food, at least when he remembered to eat.

The flight back to school was uneventful as was taking the tram home. Max, the driver, remarked that they all looked very tired.

"The moon will do that to you. Gravity changes so many things." Ron avoided mentioning robots and aliens.

"How long were you down there?" Max only monitored the systems. The computers did all the work.

Tina answered for Ron. "Just a couple of weeks. We helped break down the engineering base down there."

"See anything fun?"

Ron looked at Yana who in turn looked at Tina. "Not a whole lot. We checked out where man first walked on the moon and did some walking ourselves. It's dusty and very dark most of the time."

Max looked at the kids with a funny look. "Sounds boring."

"It sort of was. Team BMW showed us around, and we got some hands-on experience with tech, but that's about it." Ron smiled at Tina.

Sensing that they might be hiding something Max stopped asking questions, but made a silent note to mention it to the administrators. His job was to watch for irregularities.

The tram slowed to a halt in front of the entrance to the Academy. "All ashore that's going ashore. This is where you get off."

Thanking Max as they stepped off, the kids entered the

doors as a group, not as individuals. Max watched with silent interest. Something down there made this group into a cohesive team in a very short amount of time.

Diane and Dorene were waiting in the lobby for Alpha Team to return.

Diane spoke first. "Did you kids have a good time on the moon? Did Marcus and the others manage to teach you something?"

Both Ron and Tina giggled for a moment and glanced at the others. Yana cleared her throat. "Yes, Ma'am. We did. Marcus is a good teacher as well as a demonstrator. Even Bobcat taught us something." Nestor stifled a laugh at that comment.

Diane pursed her lips and frowned. "Good. You still have a couple of weeks with them. Do they have a project for you to do?"

Yana continued to answer for the group. "Yes. Marcus said we would be helping with the ten-passenger Pod project."

"Did you get a tour of the moon?" This came from Dorene.

"We did. They allowed us to use the moon rovers and we explored a little. Marcus showed us some of the craters." Yana smiled at the twin.

"Great. Do you think the next class to work with them will have as much fun as you did?"

The entire Alpha team froze for just a moment. Maxim spoke up for the rest. "We, uh, finished dismantling the base down there. The next group might only get a pod tour. The rovers were destroyed in a slight accident, so they can't be used anymore."

"Really? What happened?" Both twins' laser focused in

on the kids' expressions.

"They were crushed. Large chunks of moon rock and metal fell on them. Total accident. Bobcat and Marcus forgot they were parked there." Nestor chuckled and nudged his cousin. Maxim turned and glared at him.

"I see. Was anyone injured?" Diane didn't look happy.

"No, we were too far away from the event. It was just an accident." Maxim smiled at the twin administrators.

"OK. Well, it's getting late. You can tell us more in the morning. Get some rest." The two ladies watched as the team split up at the top of the stairs and went to the dorms.

"They're lying about something," Diane said to the open air.

"Ya think? I told better lies than that to Mom." Dorene shook her head.

"Mom was smart, you needed to. Should we confront Bozo and the other two to find out the truth?"

"Heh. You called him Bozo. Let's wait. They're kids. Most can't keep a secret to save their own lives. Whatever it is we will find out soon enough." Dorene gave her sister a nudge just because.

The next morning it was business as usual. Many of the other teams were surprised to see the Alphas were in the dining hall and told them as much.

"When did you guys get back?" Paul was one of Ron's old friends from Colorado.

"Last night. The moonbase is all dismantled and ready for demolition. We came back to help with one of BMWs pod projects."

ALPHA CLASS

"That is so cool, Ron! How was the moon?" Paul high fived Ron.

"It was pretty cool. We moon walked and got a cool tour. What has your group been doing?" Ron grinned back at his high school friend.

"We've been working with ADAM and the hackers under his command. Most of us in Echo Team only use computers, not program them, but we've been pouring over databases and matching up money and resources to countries. Really high-tech stuff. I had no idea the world was as big as it is. You being you, will know more about what they do when you get there. So far it's been really interesting."

"That's good. How are the other members of your team doing? Is it starting to feel cohesive, like a real team?" Maxim and Nestor perked up and stared at Paul.

"What do you mean by that, Ron? It's just a bunch of guys in my class. I don't hang with them or anything, if that's what you are saying." Maxim caught Ron's attention and shook his head.

Ron smiled at his friend. "It was just a question. I wondered if you bonded with anyone or something. Forget it. Have you seen any of the old gang?"

Paul smiled and launched into a huge dialog about high school and friends from the tech classes. Nestor glanced at his cousin and muttered under his breath. "Not a team yet. Are we the only ones so far?"

Maxim could only shrug as an answer. He would have to ask Ron for his observations later, but it was looking as though only they were the ones to bond with each other.

"Have you guys seen the confirmed and locked in assignments for the next round of classes?" Tina and Yana slid into the seat interrupting Ron's conversation.

"They're out already?" Ron pulled out his tablet and began scrolling. Paul looked from the girls to Ron and shook his head as he wandered off.

"Yana caught it just as they went up." Tina leaned over and pointed at Ron's tablet.

"Wow. Ok, we are confirmed to have Jeo and orbital engineering and construction. It's good we know how the suits work now. I suspect we will be in them a bunch."

"Ron, who is this Jeo?" Maxim and Nestor had their tablets out as well.

"He built the Queen's ship as well as this base. He's brilliant. This should be fun. Delta team has him this term. Roger Cook, over there told me they learned about Earth engineering first then they moved on to space." Ron smiled at his friend.

"Ah. I remember him now. Sounds exciting. Not a robot in sight." Maxim tried to laugh his slip away.

Tina glared at him to stop it. They had made the deal in good faith and she at least intended to keep it. The Queen wouldn't find out from her group for a while.

"Do you think we got away with it?"

"If you don't stop talking about it, we won't. You just can't keep a secret, can you?" William screwed the last turn on the decoration for the wall of the bar.

"What do you think?" William directed Bobcat's eyes up at the space above the bar.

Two robotic arms were crossed under the words 'Death before Dishonor.'

"It's a bit obvious. What do we say if anyone asks?"

"Deny everything. Best solution there is." William folded his arms and stared out of the window towards where Earth would be if they could see it.

"It depends upon what you deny that matters." Both Bobcat and William turned toward the new voice behind them.

Barnabas, the leader of the Queen's Rangers and her Judge, Jury, and Executioner sat at the bar.

"I would like a glass of your very best Tequila, please." The fact that Barnabas was an ancient vampire didn't faze William or Bobcat at all.

His mind-reading capabilities, however, did.

William slipped behind the bar and poured him a drink. "We've never seen you in here before, Barnabas. I didn't know you drank."

"I don't. Not really. We had to take care of a problem for the Queen, and I added another judgment to my soul." He downed the shot in one large gulp.

"Did you need another one? We were going to close up the bar and get back to work." Bobcat's hand was shaking just a bit. Inside, he was screaming and trying to sing Christmas carols to break up his thoughts.

"I'm good. Thank you, gentlemen." Barnabas left the bar humming Jingle-Bells as he walked.

"Do you think he read our minds?" Bobcat looked at William.

William pursed his lips, "What do you think?"

"That we're dead," Bobcat nodded his head, "We are so dead…"

"He doesn't always tell the Queen everything. That's what the rumor mill says anyway." William tried to calm Bobcat down.

"Maybe he won't tell her."

PAUL AND ANDERLE

The Queen was dressed to kill, literally. John Grimes, as well as Ashur, were wakened from a dead sleep and told to get dressed by Bethany Anne.

"What's wrong? Is there an attack?" John was up and dressed using his vampire-enhanced speed.

"No. Worse." BA stormed out of her quarters and into the hall. It was third shift, and there were very few staff and other workers around.

John stepped in front of his Queen. "BA, what's worse than an attack?" John had his hand on his Jean Dukes Special.

"Someone has failed to explain the truth. Hold on." She grabbed Ashur and John and went through the Etheric to just outside Team BMW's workshop.

Not bothering to say anything, ADAM communicated with Meredith and the doors into their workshop were already opened and waiting for her to walk through. She called out in her command voice, "Bobcat get your ass out here right now!"

AUTHOR NOTES: TS (SCOTT) PAUL

Written December 29, 2016

My name is TS Paul and I write Science Fiction and Paranormal.

This book brings me full circle as an author. Way back at the beginning of this year, 2016, I met and befriended an author. His name was Michael Anderle. I became a Beta reader for him and helped to edit his books and I still do to this day.

But *that* is another story.

Michael started to bug me about writing my own series of books. His theory was that I was well read, could string two sentences together, and told good stories. Why not publish?

So he told me over and over to write and to publish. So I did.

(Edit - No I didn't, his wife Heather told him over and over he should write stories. I actually told him a few times. I'm getting the credit when she put in the ten years of effort. I need to make this abundantly clear as I'm expecting to meet her in 2017 and I understand she can have a mean right hook...No...no... I actually don't know anything about a right hook, but she sounds like she could be a handful so better to fess up now rather than wait for a few months and pay, then!)

I wrote a small 13,000 word book called the Forgotten Engineer and we put it up on Amazon. It sold a few books the very first day!

So Michael told me to write another one. And then yet another one. In the course of 20 days I put out three in a series.

In November, Michael approached me and asked if I would like to write a Young Adult themed spin-off series set inside his Kurtherian Gambit series. I, of course, said Yes, of course I would!

The Etheric Academy was born. This is my first co-written project ever and so far the project has been an adventure.

AUTHOR NOTES:
MICHAEL ANDERLE

Written December 30, 2016

As always, can I say with a HUGE amount of appreciation how much it means to me that you not only read this book, but you are reading these notes as well?

This is now the …uhhhh… (The Author is counting on his fingers) Justin Sloan, Craig Martelle, Natalie Grey, mine and now Scott's… fifth author note I've done in December.

D@MN!

Now, If I write the one for Paul C. Middleton tomorrow, I'll have written six in December… SWEEET!

The plan is this book launches tomorrow, let's pray that happens (are you listening, Amazon gods?)

Scott is right, I did approach him to write a YA novel in the Kurtherian Universe because:

1) I wanted something that was more approachable for both younger audiences and those who, shall we say, prefer not to read the rather humorous but very coarse language used in the main series with Bethany Anne.

2) Anyone who follows me on Facebook knows I can't write a story without s metric s#it-ton of cussing in it… <— See! Guilty right there.

3) Scott was writing YA since last February and doing very, very well.

The thing is, I didn't expect him to say yes. Why? He has two of his own very successful series and one of them, The Federal Witch series, is blowing up HUGE. So, I figured I had better ask him, because I didn't want him to think I hadn't considered him but I wasn't expecting him to agree for the reason(s) I just mentioned.

But he did, and like he mentioned in his Author Notes, life has a way of coming around full circle.

So, Welcome TS Paul into the Kurtherian Universe with The Etheric Academy Series. May it last for the 30 potential books we see and then some!

Best Regards,
Michael Anderle

CHEF VAN NORMAN'S BORSCHT RECIPE

How to make Salt Cabbage

Measure out half a pint of shredded cabbage and half a pint of shredded carrot. Add a small amount of caraway seed and 1 tsp of salt. Using your hands mix it thoroughly. Allow the juices to flow out. Place it in a dish and cover with plastic. Allow to sit at room temperature for 2 days.

1. Place 2 pounds of lamb** in a soup pot. (Lamb Shoulder is best) Fill the pot halfway with water and bring to a boil. Reduce heat to a simmer for one hour.

2. Add five diced red potatoes and either the salt cabbage or a mixed pint of Cabbage and carrots. Simmer for 10 minutes.

3. In a separate pan Saute a large white onion in a small pan until it achieves a golden color. Add this to the soup pot.

4. Remove the Lamb and set aside

5. Shred, grate, or chop a large beet. This is for texture. The beets are to be soft. Add to pot and continue to simmer

6. Add a bay leaf. Salt and pepper to taste

7. Chop two cups of fresh parsley and put in the pot.

8. Add a half cup of fresh dill and 1 tablespoon of lemon juice to the pot

9. Chop the Lamb into cubes and return to the pot along with any juices. Simmer 10 minutes

10. Serve in bowl with a dollop of sour cream in the middle topped with fresh parsley. A hearty rye or black bread make this a meal

**You can use Pork Shoulder, Ham, or Bacon (pork belly) in place of the Lamb. But Lamb is traditional. Cook times will vary if using an alternate meat.

.

COMING JANUARY/
FEBRUARY 2017

NEVER
SUBMIT
THE KURTHERIAN GAMBIT 15

MICHAEL ANDERLE

TS PAUL

THE ATHENA LEE CHRONICLES

Book 0 - The Lost Pilot
Book 1 – Forgotten Engineer
Book 2 – Engineering Murder
Book 3 - Ghost Ships of Terra
Book 4 - Revolutionary
Book 5 – Insurrection
Book 6 – Imperial Subversion
Book 7 - The Martian Inheritance
Book 8 - Infiltration
Book 9 - Prelude to War
Book 9.5 - Uncommon Life
Book 10 - War to the Knife
Ghosts of Noodlemass Past

ATHENA LEE UNIVERSE

Shades of Learning
Space Cadets (1st Quarter 2017)

SHORT STORY COLLECTIONS

Wilson's War
A Colony of CATT's

THE FEDERAL WITCH SERIES

Book 0 – Born a Witch - Drafted by the FBI
Book 1 – Magical Probi
Book 2 - Conjuring Quantico
Book 3 - Special Agent in Charge (1st Quarter 2017)
Book 4 - Witness Enchantment (2nd Quarter 2017)
Night of the Unicorn (TBD)
Cat's Night Out and Other Tales (Jan 2017)

THE ETHERIC ACADEMY

Book 1 – Alpha Team 01 - Team BMW
Book 2 – Alpha Team 02 - Jeo & Peter (2017)
Book 3 - Alpha Team 03 (2017)

BOX SETS and OTHER

Chronicles of Athena Lee Books 01-03
Chronicles of Athena Lee Books 04-06
Chronicles of Athena Lee Books 07-09
The Federal Witch Book 01 Books 00-02

MICHAEL ANDERLE

KURTHERIAN GAMBIT SERIES
TITLES INCLUDE:

First Arc

Death Becomes Her (01) - Queen Bitch (02) - Love Lost (03) - Bite This (04)
Never Forsaken (05) - Under My Heel (06) Kneel Or Die (07)

Second Arc

We Will Build (08) - It's Hell To Choose (09) - Release The Dogs of War (10)
Sued For Peace (11) - We Have Contact (12) - My Ride is a Bitch (13)
Don't Cross This Line (14)

Third Arc (Due 2017)

Never Submit (15) - Never Surrender (16) - Forever Defend (17)
Might Makes Right (18) - Ahead Full (19) - Capture Death (20)
Life Goes On (21)

TERRY HENRY "TH" WALTON CHRONICLES
* With Craig Martelle *

Nomad Found (01)
Nomad Redeemed (02)
Jan 2017

SHORT STORIES

Frank Kurns Stories of the Unknownworld 01 (7.5)
You Don't Mess with John's Cousin

Frank Kurns Stories of the Unknownworld 02 (9.5)
Bitch's Night Out

Frank Kurns Stories of the Unknownworld 02 (13.25)
With Natalie Grey
Bellatrix

ANTHOLOGIES

Glimpse
Honor in Death
(Michael's First Few Days)

Beyond the Stars: At Galaxy's Edge
Tabitha's Vacation

TS PAUL
SOCIAL

Website:
https://tspaul.blogspot.com

GoodReads and BookBub
https://www.bookbub.com/authors/t-s-paul

https://www.goodreads.com/author/
show/15054219.T_S_Paul

Facebook Here:
https://www.facebook.com/ForgottenEngineer/

MICHAEL ANDERLE SOCIAL

Website:
http://kurtherianbooks.com/

Email List:
http://kurtherianbooks.com/email-list/

Facebook Here:
https://www.facebook.com/
TheKurtherianGambitBooks/

Made in the USA
Middletown, DE
01 April 2021

36735071R00113